WITHDRAWN
Love
and Lizzie

Rosie Rushton lives in Northampton. She is a governor of the local Church of England secondary school, a licensed lay minister and passionate about all issues relating to young people. Her hobbies include learning Swahili, travelling, going to the theatre, reading, walking, being juvenile with her grandchildren and playing hopscotch when no one is looking. Her ambitions are to write the novel that has been pounding in her brain for years but never quite made it to the keyboard, to visit China and learn to sing in tune.

Other 21st Century Austens, by Rosie Rushton:
The Secrets of Love
Summer of Secrets
Secret Schemes and Daring Dreams

Love, Lies and Lizzie

Rosie Rushton

Piccadilly Press • London

First published in Great Britain in 2009
by Piccadilly Press Ltd,
5 Castle Road, London NW1 8PR
www.piccadillypress.co.uk

A catalogue record for this book is available from the British Library

ISBN: 978 1 85340 979 0 (paperback)

1 3 5 7 9 10 8 6 4 2

Printed in the UK by CPI Bookmarque, Croydon, CR0 4TD
Cover illustration by Susan Hellard
Cover design by Simon Davis
Text design by Carolyn Griffiths, Cambridge
Set in Goudy and Caslon

It is a truth universally acknowledged that no author can produce a book without a myriad host of supporters nagging, cajoling, encouraging, and providing chocolate cake in the background. Therefore my heartfelt thanks are due, yet again, to Celia Rees for nagging this book into existence; to Andrew, Eunice and Nicola Willis for their advice on Figeac and head injuries; to Sarah and Ros Martin for cake and literary comment; to the girls of Year 9LBY of Northampton School for Girls for putting me straight about the current teen scene; and to my wonderful, patient editor, Ruth Williams, and my equally wonderful, patient agent, Jane Judd.

PART ONE

CHAPTER 1

'On first entering the neighbourhood . . .'
(Jane Austen, *Pride and Prejudice*)

'SO YOU DUMPED HIM? JUST LIKE THAT? IN THE MIDDLE OF the school trip? Are you crazy?'

'I've never been more sane,' Lizzie asserted, trundling her suitcase across the school forecourt towards the car park. 'We just don't have anything in common any more.'

'But Toby's so lovely,' her older sister Jane protested. 'Really gentle and unassuming and —'

'Boring!' Lizzie concluded, heaving the case into the boot of their mother's Polo and glancing with satisfaction at the 'P' plate tied to the back bumper. She had passed her test just two weeks earlier and still couldn't quite believe it.

'Lizzie, he's crazy about you,' Jane persisted, slipping into the driving seat and turning on the ignition.

'Sure he is, in a sloppy, spaniel puppy sort of way.' Lizzie shrugged, pulling the band off her ponytail and shaking her thick chestnut-brown hair free. 'The thing is, I'm not like you, Janey. I'm not a hearts and flowers, soft-focus type of person.'

'You can say that again,' her sister teased.

'I want more out of a relationship than a guy who agrees to do whatever I do, go wherever I say, constantly tells me he can't live without me . . .'

Jane sighed and shook her head. 'Most of us would cross continents to find a boyfriend like that,' she stressed, flicking her ash-blond hair behind her ears and adjusting the driving mirror. 'And you get one and chuck him away.'

'Sorry.' Lizzie guessed from the sudden flush of colour to Jane's pale cheeks that she was thinking about Simon, the only real boyfriend she had had in nineteen years, the guy she'd been head over heels in love with – until six weeks earlier, when she found out that he was not only two-timing her while she was away at uni, but even posting jokey updates on MySpace. 'I didn't mean to . . .'

'It's OK, I'm so over it,' Jane assured her, not very convincingly. 'Hey, do you want to drive?'

Lizzie shook her head. 'I'm shattered,' she admitted. 'And Friday rush hour isn't quite the best time to start.'

'No probs,' her sister replied. 'So when are you going to tell Mum?'

'Tell her what?'

'That you and Toby have split, silly,' Jane replied, accelerating out of the school car park and down the hill towards the Meryton ring road, busy with traffic. 'You know how she adores him.'

'Adores the fact that he's got a double-barrelled surname and a father who's an MP more like,' Lizzie pointed out with a wry smile. 'You know what she's like.'

'Tell me about it,' Jane said. 'She's been even worse since we moved house. You'll never guess the latest.'

'Go on,' groaned Lizzie.

'Well, two days after I got back from uni – the day you left on the trip, come to think of it – she started going round the whole village, knocking on people's doors and introducing herself. Can you believe that? And there was me hoping she was going to keep a low profile.'

'Mum?' Lizzie laughed, relieved at the chance to change the subject. 'Low profile? That's like saying you expect Dad to turn into a party goer!'

The girls' father was the kind of guy who, given half a chance, would have gone through life in a cloak of invisibility.

'Yes, and talking of Dad . . . oh no, I'm in the wrong lane. I keep thinking we still live at the old house.'

'It's odd, isn't it?' Lizzie sighed. 'I still can't get my head around everything that's happened.'

For as long as the girls could remember, home had been a three-storey and somewhat dilapidated, turn-of-the-century semi on the eastern side of Meryton (which, as Lizzie's mother kept reminding them, had quite the wrong postcode and got a whiff of the sewage works in neighbouring Eckford every time the wind was in a northerly direction). It had been the home of Lizzie's paternal grandparents and to say it showed signs of wear and tear was an understatement. For years, Lizzie's social-climbing mother had spent her weekends inspecting show homes on all the new village developments within a twenty-mile radius of the town, even assuring the rather bored-looking sales reps in the mobile site offices that she was definitely a genuine interested party and not a time-waster.

'I don't understand why you put yourself through all this,' her long-suffering husband would protest every time she waxed lyrical about the conservatories on the new Georgian-style houses at Hunters Park, or the slate floors and oak units in the gigantic kitchens of the new riverside houses in Lower Grendon. 'In case you've forgotten, we have five daughters to clothe, feed and put through university. Stop wasting your time.'

'*You've got to have a dream, if you don't have a dream, how you gonna have a dream come true?*' Lizzie's mum would trill. (As well as being addicted to house-hunting, she was very into old musicals. However, while Lizzie had inherited her grandmother's perfect pitch, Mrs Bennet had not.)

After each of his wife's house-hunting afternoons, Mr Bennet would sigh, raise his eyebrows and retreat to his den (which was actually the converted garage) to immerse himself in his collection of poetry books, and play Wagner as loudly as he dared.

But then, two days after Easter, everything had changed. Totally out of the blue, Aloysius Hull had died and left Mrs Bennet his entire estate, just under two million pounds. Lizzie's mother hadn't a clue who Aloysius Hull was until the solicitor acting for his estate informed her that he happened, in fact, to be her second cousin, three times removed (or was it third cousin, twice removed?), a reclusive bachelor in his nineties who had lived in a rambling house in the wilds of

Scotland, had no family and who remembered Alice Bennet when she was Alice Frognall, aged five, 'a charming child,' (according to his will) 'who shared her bag of jelly babies with me when she visited with her family, the rest of whom were idiots'. (The solicitor apologised for including this last sentence in his letter, but as he explained, the law demanded complete and full disclosure of the deceased's words and wishes. He need not have worried: Alice's opinion of her relatives agreed with his wholeheartedly.)

'We can do it, finally we can do it!' Lizzie's mother had cried, after she had stopped shrieking, dancing round the kitchen and waving the solicitor's letter in everyone's face. 'Oh, Harry, we can, we really can!'

She had hurled herself into the arms of her bemused husband and hugged him.

'Can do what?' he had asked, a little pink around the mouth from all the excitement. 'Change the car? Get surround sound? That new Sony system?'

'Buy the house at Longbourn Oaks, of course!' Alice had replied, her plump cheeks flushed with excitement. 'It's perfect – oh, this is meant to be, I know it is!'

'Great!' exclaimed fifteen-year-old Katie, who was at the stage of her verbal development that limited most of her conversation to one-liners – partly because she considered it far more cool than using complete sentences, and partly because her twin sister Lydia rarely allowed her to get more than a word in edgeways.

'Great? Living in some poxy village in the middle of nowhere?' Lydia had burst out at once. 'God, Katie, you are so sad. No way am I moving from town – like, what would that do to my social life?'

'Actually, it would be brilliant – we could grow vegetables, and keep bees, and go totally organic,' seventeen-year-old Meredith had declared. 'I'd like that.'

'Yes, well you would,' Lydia snapped. 'Since you don't have a life and think that recycling a paper bag is the height of excitement.'

'For heaven's sake, will you all just stop this nonsense?' their father, Harry, had interrupted. 'There is absolutely no way we are going to squander this windfall on some crumbling country cottage with woodworm and —'

'I'm not talking about somewhere old, you silly man,' his wife protested. 'This one is on that new development – Priory Park – the one that backs on to the golf course. The moment I saw it I knew it was the house for us.'

'Even worse,' Harry retorted. 'Overpriced, pretentious . . .' He paused, eyeing his wife anxiously. 'What do you mean – the moment you saw it you knew?'

Triumphantly, Alice had produced a glossy brochure from the kitchen drawer and thrust it under his nose.

'Isn't it beautiful? And it's only nine hundred thousand, so we can afford it and still have plenty of money over.'

'Nine hundred thous—! No way,' Harry had blustered, glancing briefly at the array of coloured photographs. 'This isn't our type of place at all.'

'It's exactly our type of place,' Alice retorted. 'There are seven bedrooms, and four reception rooms.'

'Who needs four?'

'You do, darling,' Lizzie's mother said sweetly. 'You could soundproof one and have it as a music room.'

The only time that Alice Bennet employed anything approaching subtlety was when attempting to manipulate her husband.

'Well, I . . .' For an instant he hesitated, clearly entranced at the thought of *The Ring Cycle* playing at full volume and blotting out what he always referred to as the twittering of his teenage daughters.

'And just think, we'd only be a couple of miles from the Lucases,' she went on triumphantly. The Lucases and the Bennets had been friends for years, and Emily was Lizzie's best mate. 'Don't forget, Geoff is a member of the Oaks golf club – he could get you in.'

If she had stopped there and then, she might have won her husband over a lot faster. Sadly, a measured conversation was not one of Alice's talents.

'And we'd have enough space for the girls to invite their friends to stay over without having to sleep on the floor,' she concluded happily.

'Ye gods, do you really think I can cope with any more adolescent hormones round the place?' he groaned. 'Alice, this is a crazy idea and it's not going to happen. For one thing, the village is way over the other side of town, quite the wrong place for getting to my office.'

'It's in precisely the right place for people in our new position,' Alice argued. 'Longbourn Oaks was in the *Sunday Times* property supplement as one of the top ten desirable rural locations.'

'And that's supposed to impress me?'

'And *HomeHunter* magazine called it "*modern living with the elegance of a bygone age*", his wife stressed impatiently. 'Residents can use all the facilities of Longbourn Country Club – pool and jacuzzi and everything, and the ruins of Longbourn Priory are still standing on the edge of the new golf course, you know . . . you'd like that, you like history . . .'

'Hey, that's very romantic,' Lydia had exclaimed, momentarily forgetting her objections to shifting from town. 'Do you reckon the whole place is haunted by the ghosts of frustrated nuns who died desperate for the sight of a man?'

'Which is something you're never likely to do,' Meredith had muttered, glaring at her sister so fiercely that her bushy eyebrows met. 'The way you were coming on to Jake Martin the other night!'

'Just because I have sex appeal and you don't.'

'I'd rather have a few brain cells – not that you'd know anything about those!'

'Your wonderful brain doesn't actually teach you how to pull though, does it?'

'Will you two stop it right now!' Their mother, while not being exactly narrow-minded (a mother of five children has to admit to a vague knowledge of matters sexual), liked to pretend that her younger children were still mere innocents in the matter of human relations. While this was true of Meredith, who insisted that she had never met a guy worth a second glance, it could not be said of Lydia, whose first sentence at the age of fourteen months had been 'Kiss me' and who had seen no reason to change her priorities in the intervening years.

'Yes, let's stop this whole ridiculous discussion,' their father added, 'and start talking sense for a change. We could certainly paint the house, buy a few new bits and pieces, even have a holiday, maybe in Italy, visit a few opera houses . . .'

'Considering,' Lizzie's mother had replied icily, 'that it was my generosity with the jelly babies that brought this legacy about in the first place, and that the money was left specifically to *me*, I rather think it's up to *me* to decide how it's spent, don't you, dear?'

Four months later, the paperwork was complete and the house was theirs. They had moved in the day that Lizzie's A-levels finished.

'So, how was the choir trip?' Jane broke in on Lizzie's thoughts a bit later as they headed for the village. 'Aside from you breaking Toby's heart, that is?'

'It went OK,' Lizzie replied, ignoring her sister's last remark and desperately trying to blot the memory of the blazing row with her now ex-boyfriend the night before the tour ended. 'Five concerts in seven days was a bit full on, though. I had three solos and now my voice is knackered.'

'That's a shame,' teased Jane. 'Mum's already sucked up to the new vicar and said you'll sing in the church choir.'

'I wish she'd stop interfering with my life!' Lizzie burst out. 'She is such a control freak – like I'm really going to ditch St Peter's for this new place.'

Lizzie was not only her school's star soprano, but also the leading light in Voices Raised, a kids' and teen choir she had got going when she was fifteen because, as she had pointed out to the vicar, not everyone wanted to hear ancient hymns sung by ancient people with wavering voices. As her mind darted back to her church in the centre of Meryton, the scheme that had been taking root in her mind all week exploded once more into the forefront of her brain.

'Honestly, Jane, you are so lucky to be at uni and not have Mum breathing down your neck day and night.'

The instant the words were out she regretted them.

'Well, you could have been going in October, if you hadn't opted for a gap year,' Jane commented, turning down the slip road into the village. 'Have you decided what you're going to do for the next twelve months?'

'Um – not yet. You must admit, this is a pretty village, isn't it?' Lizzie murmured, gesturing towards the first row of thatched cottages on the approach to the duck pond.

'You are changing the subject,' Jane countered. 'And your nose is twitching, which means you're in a state. What's up?'

'Nothing,' Lizzie said, as brightly as she could, unwilling even to try to verbalise all her conflicting thoughts and emotions. 'Just tired. And I guess . . . Hey! Isn't that Lydia?'

Jane slowed down and peered through the windscreen.

'What the hell is she doing?' she gasped.

Their fifteen-year-old sister, dressed in the tiniest pair of denim shorts and a sequinned vest top, was sitting on a low wall beside the entrance to the churchyard. Her arms were hooked round the neck of a suntanned guy with a sun-bleached crew cut, and her lips were fastened to his as if by Super Glue.

'Who is that guy?' Lizzie asked Jane as she pulled up at the side of the road.

'Never seen him before in my life,' her sister replied. 'Should we call out to her, do you think?'

'Too right we should,' Lizzie nodded, zapping the window. 'Lydia! Hi, Lydia!'

Their sister turned round, jumped off the wall and, grabbing the guy by the hand, dragged him over to the car.

'Hiya,' she said cheerfully. 'Cool timing – we need a lift.'

'You what?'

'A lift,' Lydia said calmly. 'We need to get into town – only Denny's bike's off the road – this is Denny, by the way.'

'Does Mum know what you're doing?' Lizzie demanded.

'Lizzie!' Lydia coloured and threw her sister a murderous look. 'I'm not a kid. Anyway, what's it to you? Will you give us a lift or not?'

'Not,' Jane cut in. 'Lizzie's only just got back.'

'So? You can drop her home and then take us and —'

'Lyddy – no!' Jane said.

'It's no big deal,' Denny remarked easily, glancing at his watch. He turned to Lydia. 'What do you say I see you at the club later for a swim, babe, yeah? Say about seven?'

'You bet! Can't wait to see you with your kit off!' Lydia giggled, blowing him a kiss and opening the rear door of the car.

'Who is that guy?' Lizzie demanded, the instant Jane pulled away from the kerb. 'He looks way older than you.'

'Oh God, Lizzie, don't start!' Lydia said, pulling a face. 'He's nineteen, OK?'

'So how long have you known him? Where did you meet him?' Jane demanded.

'What's with all the questions?' Lydia snapped, scooping her long hair into a scrunchie. 'Like it's any of your business.'

She pulled the wrapper off a piece of chewing gum and stuffed it into her mouth.

'If you must know, I met him yesterday,' she said smugly. 'He lives —'

'Yesterday?' Lizzie blurted out, as Jane turned the car into the paved driveway of their house. 'And you're snogging him today. Lydia, you are such a tart.'

'No I'm not, I'm just irresistible,' Lydia said laughing, totally unconcerned at her sister's censure. 'Denny says I kiss like —'

'I don't want to know,' Lizzie interjected.

'You're in a mood,' Lydia remarked. 'Pining for the sainted Toby, are you? How sweet!'

'Lydia?'

'Yeah?'

'Shut up.'

CHAPTER 2

'Lizzie has something more of quickness than her sisters.'
(Jane Austen, *Pride and Prejudice*)

THE VILLAGE OF LONGBOURN OAKS, EIGHT MILES FROM the ever-expanding market town of Meryton, dated back to the tenth century; it boasted a Saxon church, two pubs (The Gardiner's Arms, which the locals favoured, and The Artichoke, which they avoided like the plague), a post office and general store and the locally famous Barn Theatre (a converted cowshed), home to the Longbourn Players.

None of this was of the remotest interest to Lydia Bennet. Two things had converted her in the space of twenty-four hours from being sullen, surly and totally opposed to living in what she called the back of beyond. The first was the fact that the mother of her best friend, Amber Forster, had just shacked up with her new man in the neighbouring village; the second was the discovery that just half a mile outside the village on the road to Pitswell stood Longbourn College of Equine Studies. It wasn't the horses that appealed to Lydia; for her its greatest attraction was that at least two-thirds of the students were male.

'Denny's dad's the principal,' she had informed her sisters on the way home. 'They live in this huge bungalow in the grounds. Anyway, Denny says loads of the final year students are hanging out round here for summer holiday placements, and riding in shows and stuff. There's this guy Zak, I met him last night too, he's got a quad bike and he says he'll take me off-roading next week. Then there's Tim, Denny's best mate – he's got his own horses and he's really fit and he'll be around all summer helping design the new cross-country course and Amber really fancies him, but I think . . .'

She had babbled on relentlessly until Jane turned into the driveway of their new home. Priory Park, an exclusive development of nine houses, was built on what had once been Priory Home Farm, until the owners realised that building houses for aspirational homeowners was a lot more lucrative than attempting to cope with government cutbacks. It was planned as a figure of eight, so that none of the houses had the ignominy of a garden that backed on to anyone else's, but all overlooked either the newly designed eighteen-hole golf course to the west, the Longbourn woods with the eponymous oak trees to the north and east, or the River Mere to the south.

The Bennets' double-fronted house, constructed of locally reclaimed creamy coloured stone, stood at the end of the cul-de-sac. Built in an L-shape, it had huge picture windows, wide chimneys and not one, but two conservatories. There was a small one jutting out from the side of the house, and a much larger one at the rear which Mrs Bennet insisted on calling the morning room.

This wasn't because she chose to eat her muesli there each day, but because Geneva Jevington had written an article in the *Independent* stating quite emphatically that the morning room was enjoying a revival among those for whom gracious living was second nature.

However, as Lizzie trundled her suitcase through the heavy oak front door and into the hallway, still smelling of fresh paint, the atmosphere was anything but gracious. Before she could draw breath, her youngest sister, Katie, came careering down the stairs, her face like thunder.

'You cow! You went out without me!' she shouted, pushing past Lizzie and grabbing Lydia's arm. 'You swore that if I did your geography homework, I could come too.'

'Oh, get stuffed! Like I really want to nursemaid you for the rest of my life,' Lydia retorted.

At which Katie promptly burst into tears. Katie did that a lot. In fact, for twins born within seven minutes of one another, Lydia and Katie could not have been more different. Lydia, fifteen going on twenty-five, was one of those girls who truly believed that the world owed her a living. She didn't give a toss about school work, or indeed any kind of rule or regulation, she changed her hair colour on a monthly basis – it was currently a rather overpowering shade of russet with what the packet called 'corn cob highlights' – and she had an innate sense of style, bolstered by an unwavering confidence in her own magnetic charms. Her mother said that of all her daughters, Lydia would go the furthest; her father said that he was sure she was right, it was just that he worried in which direction she would head.

'You are always so horrid to me!' Katie wailed as Lydia shrugged her off impatiently. Katie, of course, was also fifteen. But there the similarity ended. Where Lydia was reckless, Katie worried about everything. Lydia could eat for England and had her mother's chubby build and rosy cheeks; Katie was skinny, pale and picked at her food as if suspicious that every pea was out to poison her. Katie had just one ambition in life: to win her twin's approval. This Lydia gave very infrequently and then only when it served her own purpose.

'Oh, save your breath to cool your porridge, loser!' Lydia snapped. 'You are so juvenile!'

'Can you lot shut the hell up?' Meredith stormed out of the sitting room. 'I'm trying to listen to Eco-watch.'

Meredith was as unlike any of her sisters as it was possible to be. She had neither Jane's delicate features and flyaway blond hair, nor Lizzie's unruly chestnut curls and olive skin. She wasn't sociable like Lydia, and she certainly didn't worry about pleasing other people the way Katie did. The only characteristics she had inherited from the Bennet gene pool were her father's height and his total lack of style. Much as she adored him, Lizzie had to admit that even when dressed for the office, her six-foot-three father resembled a hat stand on to which someone had carelessly flung an assortment of garments, none of which co-ordinated and most of which appeared to be resting en route to a jumble sale. Meredith, who scoured the charity shops for clothes, was the conscience of the family – monitoring their recycling, nagging her mother whenever she bought a banana that wasn't fairly traded, and constantly turning down the thermostat on the central heating while lecturing her sisters about global warming. It was all very worthwhile and Lizzie admired her for it; but she couldn't help wishing that her sister was a bit more cheerful about it all.

'Oh, hi, Lizzie, you're back,' Meredith said, frowning and picking distractedly at a spot on the side of her nose. 'That's good, because I need you and Jane to sign this petition I've drawn up.'

She paused, as from behind the closed kitchen door all hell appeared to be breaking loose.

'How can you even think of it? Him? Here? After everything that happened?' Mrs Bennet's voice, shrill at the best of times, was getting higher and higher.

'Alice, be reasonable, it's only . . .' Lizzie heard her father murmur.

'Me? You're the one who's not being reasonable. You'll just have to say no, tell him —'

'I'll tell him he's most welcome!'

Lizzie and Jane exchanged glances. Seldom was their father that assertive, opting more often for the quiet life than facing a confrontation with his volatile wife.

'What's going on?' Lydia muttered to Lizzie.

'I think,' said Lizzie, as the kitchen door flew open, and her mother, scarlet in the face, burst into the hall, 'that we're about to find out.'

'You want to know what's going on?' their mother shouted, pushing past her husband who was standing in the doorway with a look of bewilderment on his face. 'Ask him! Oh.'

She paused, eyeing Lizzie in surprise.

'You're back. Good. Maybe you can make your father see sense.'

'Yes, thank you, I had a great time,' Lizzie commented sarcastically. 'Ask him about what exactly?'

'Hello, darling, we missed you,' her father said, blowing her a kiss. 'It's something about nothing. I had an email this morning at the office, that's all. From Drew.'

'Ah.' Lizzie sighed. It was all beginning to fall into place.

'Drew? Who's Drew?' Lydia burst into life at the mention of a boy.

'You know,' Jane reminded her. 'Dad's godson Drew. Lives in America.'

'Him? I thought he was called Andy.'

'That was when he was little,' her father explained, a faint smile flickering across his face. 'He's called himself Drew ever since he started shaving.'

'So – what about him?' Lizzie asked.

'I'll tell you what about him!' Her mother exploded into life once more. 'He's invited himself to sponge off us for a fortnight. And your father is set on letting him.'

'Alice, for God's sake!' Harry shouted. 'He's not sponging, he's —'

'Really? Well, his parents sponged so I'm sure it's in his genes,' Alice spat back. 'But of course, you never could see things even when they were under your nose and —'

She was stopped in full flood by their new, multichannel electric doorbell trilling out the first few bars of 'When the Saints Come Marching In'. Lizzie, cringing at the total naffness of her mother's choice in bells, edged gratefully towards the stairs, glad of a diversion that would let her escape to her bedroom.

'Oh my God, what if it's Denny?' Lydia cried. 'I'm nowhere near ready, I haven't done my face!'

'And I can't see anyone,' her mother blurted out. 'I'm far too distraught . . . oh!'

At that moment, Katie, clearly wanting to do anything that would stop the argument dead in its tracks, threw open the front door. Standing on the threshold, immaculate in a pair of white linen trousers and a cerise silk shirt, was a tall woman with a sheaf of papers in her hand and a somewhat bemused expression on her face.

'Oh, I have got the right house,' she declared. 'There was such a commotion going on, I thought for a moment I must be mistaken.'

'Mrs Bingley!' Had Lizzie not known her mother so well, she would have been astonished at the transformation from screeching banshee to charming lady of the house. 'You caught us in the middle of one of our silly little games – role play – it helps Katie and Lydia so much with their drama homework.'

Jane snorted quietly into her hand while Lizzie, struggling to keep composed, found herself examining in some detail the watercolour of Clayton windmill that hung on the hall wall.

'Would someone have her put down, please? Like now,' Lydia muttered, and stomped up the stairs.

'Really? How interesting.' Mrs Bingley sounded anything but interested. 'Now the thing is —'

'This is Mrs Bingley, girls,' their mother said. 'She lives at Netherfield Manor.'

Lizzie sighed inwardly at the way her mother put the emphasis on the last word.

'Hello,' Lizzie and Jane chorused obediently.

'My goodness, what a lot of you!' Mrs Bingley murmured, glancing round the hall. 'Now I can't stop, Alice, but when you called round the other day, I was so wrapped up in my preparations for our Barn Theatre fundraiser that I quite forgot to invite you to a little gathering we're having tomorrow evening. Nothing fancy – just Pimm's and canapés. I want as many people from the village as possible because . . . oh, well I can explain all that later. Now will you come? Seven o'clock sharp.'

'Mrs Bingley, I'd be thrilled,' Lizzie's mother trilled.

'Oh, call me Vanessa,' Mrs Bingley urged her graciously. 'And do feel free to bring the whole family – my two are home, and Charlie's brought a friend down for the summer – be great for you all to get together. Caroline is always moaning about having nothing to do now we've sold the Chelsea pad! Till then!'

And with that she turned and clattered down the driveway on her four-inch gold stiletto heels.

'Well, now!' Alice declared, shutting the door behind her. 'Isn't that wonderful? Pimm's and canapés – very county!' She turned to her husband. 'Isn't that nice of her to invite us?'

'Considering you have been pestering her on an almost daily basis, I assume an invitation to this party was the only way she thought she'd get any peace,' he remarked.

Lizzie grinned. She and her father shared the same sense of humour, a fact that irritated her mother beyond belief.

As Alice retreated into the kitchen, he gave Lizzie a hug. 'That'll take her mind off Drew coming, anyway.' He smiled.

'I wouldn't count on it,' Lizzie replied. 'Knowing Mum, she's only just begun.'

'Peace at last!' Lizzie said to herself ten minutes later, closing her bedroom door firmly behind her and flopping down on her bed (which had been put in quite the wrong position and which first thing tomorrow she would move under the window). Even though the new house didn't feel like home yet, it had one distinct advantage – she had a room to herself. Of course, she'd been on her own in term time before the move, but every holiday when Jane came back from Goldsmiths College, they had been forced to double up just like when they were kids. Of all her sisters, she was closest to Jane; but sharing with someone who thought a room was a tip if one pair of socks peeped out from under the bed was a strain she could do without. From now on, she could do what she liked, when she liked.

'Hey, can I come in?' Jane peered round the door. 'I need sanctuary!'

Lizzie groaned to herself and bit her tongue. 'Sure,' she said, patting the bed. 'What's up?'

'Katie's crying, because Lydia keeps baiting her; Meredith's giving out recycling target sheets; Mum's so busy yelling at Dad about Drew that she's burned half the supper and Lydia's borrowed my pink shirt and got make-up all over the collar. Need I go on?'

Lizzie threw her a sympathetic smile. 'I wonder what life would be like if Mum and Dad had got their heads around family planning,' she mused. 'I mean, I love them all but . . .'

'. . . preferably in small doses and not all at once,' Jane finished with a laugh. 'I know what you mean.' She winced slightly as a door slammed downstairs. 'This Drew thing,' she went on. 'I don't really get it. I mean, it's not like Dad's forever spending time with the guy these days. They haven't met up since he was ten and now he's what . . . twenty-two? What's the problem?'

'The problem,' Lizzie reminded her, 'is that he's Felicity's son.'

Back in the days when Lizzie's father had been at university, he and Felicity had been an item. Big time. Lizzie knew a few of the details from her dad's brother, Uncle Guy, who said that Felicity was brainy, ambitious and loaded.

'We all thought they'd get engaged the minute they graduated,' Uncle Guy had told her, 'but then along came your mum.'

That was the bit of the story that all five girls had loved best when they were small; how their mother, a student at the nearby art college, had been sitting on the pavement in Meryton town centre one Saturday afternoon, doing chalk drawings while some of her mates busked outside the library to supplement their meagre grant. What happened next was to change at least three lives forever. Lizzie's mum said it was all down to Mercury being retrograde and Venus being in the ascendant (or something like that), their dad said it was divine intervention, and what Felicity said is not repeatable. Suffice to say that at precisely three o'clock, Harry and Felicity had been charging down the High Street in the middle of a flaming row, with Felicity screeching at the top of her voice and Harry, who never liked to make an exhibition of himself, attempting to look as if he wasn't there. Felicity had belted round the corner, bumped into Alice's friend Jo, who was attempting to play 'The Entertainer' on the clarinet, and totally failed to see Alice squatting on the ground in front of her. Felicity's stiletto heel landed *smack bang* in the middle of Alice's hand and Alice, never stoical at the best of times, proceeded to faint right across her chalk drawing of Mickey Mouse in a hot-air balloon.

'That's when I fell in love with her,' Lizzie's father was fond of relating. 'She looked so white and wan and small.' (At this point the girls always giggled, since, having given birth to five children in very quick succession, their mother was now rotund, chubby cheeked and a force to be reckoned with.)

It had been Harry who called the ambulance, Harry who sat in A&E while Alice's broken hand was attended to, Harry who patiently mopped his jeans with a paper towel after Felicity had hurled a can of Coca-Cola at him and stormed out in a huff.

'He asked me out that very night,' Alice would recount proudly, 'even though I'd been sick down my skirt and smelled evil.'

'Too much information,' Meredith would mutter. (People who didn't know Meredith well were tempted to call her Merry; people who did never bothered, because frankly, she was anything but. Lizzie constantly told her to lighten up, Jane tried to be kind and say that it was just that Meredith found life challenging, and Meredith said that life wasn't the problem, it was the rest of her family.)

'I think,' her Uncle Guy had whispered to Lizzie at her sixteenth birthday party, when recounting the story for the umpteenth time, 'that your parents getting together was the main reason your grandparents decided to sell up and buy a condo in Puerto Banus. They had their hearts set on your dad marrying Felicity – but she was a total snob and I think Harry was well out of it.'

He had winked at her, knowing full well that when it came to snobbery, Alice Bennet could give anyone a run for their money.

'You have to admit,' Lizzie said to Jane now, hurling a cushion on to the floor and stretching out on the bed, 'it would have been a whole heap easier for Mum if Felicity had just disappeared off the scene, instead of stalking Dad for months, and then marrying his best mate – what was he called? Something bizarre.'

'Ambrose,' Jane replied. 'Like the creamed rice.'

'That's it,' Lizzie said laughing. 'And then they all decided to go into business together, so Felicity's forever under Mum's nose.'

'And more to the point, under Dad's,' added Jane. 'You have to admit Dad was slightly lacking on the tact and discretion front.'

'He should never have agreed to be godfather to their kid,' Lizzie nodded. 'I mean, that was bound to wind Mum up.'

'It wouldn't have been so bad if Ambrose hadn't made Dad co-guardian of the baby in the event of his death,' Jane remarked, 'and then gone and promptly died. Though, to be fair, I don't imagine that Ambrose actually planned the dying bit. Or leaving the business in such a mess.'

'True,' Lizzie nodded. 'But honestly, why has Andy – sorry, Drew – come out of the woodwork after all this time? I thought once his mother remarried and went to live in America, that was that. Dad sent birthday and Christmas presents – end of story.'

'Don't know,' Jane shrugged. 'Guess we'll find out over supper – assuming there's enough unburned bits to go round.'

'I don't want supper,' Lydia announced half an hour later. 'I'm off out.'

'But darling, you've been out all day,' her mother began, pulling off her apron and tossing it to one side. 'Where were you? Shopping?'

'No way – I was out pulling,' Lydia laughed. 'What's more, I reckon I scored!'

'You are a little monkey,' her mother sighed affectionately, ruffling Lydia's hair.

Jane and Lizzie exchanged exasperated glances. It never failed to astonish them that Lydia could get away with behaviour that would have resulted in a week's grounding if either of *them* had tried it on. But then

Lydia was their mother's favourite: unlike most parents, who try to conceal their preferences when it comes to their offspring, Alice had always blatantly favoured Lydia and, far from disapproving of her wayward behaviour, seemed almost proud of it.

'I don't think you should be going anywhere, Lydia,' her father interjected. 'Sit down and eat your supper.'

'No way! It's all arranged – I told Denny.'

'So unarrange it,' her father replied. 'You can see your school friends any day of the week.'

'School friend? Get real – like, I'd really go out with one of those losers,' Lydia replied scathingly. 'Denny's not from school, he's at uni and he's got a summer job working for his dad.'

'I don't care if he's employed as senior footman at Buckingham Palace,' her father said. 'Sit!'

'If you don't let me go, I'll just die,' Lydia whined.

'Promise?' muttered Meredith.

'Mum, tell him,' Lydia pleaded, sticking her tongue out at her sister.

'Well, I suppose if your father says . . .' Alice began.

'And what's more,' Mr Bennet went on, somewhat ill-advisedly, 'when Drew arrives, we're going to have proper, leisurely family meals, with no histrionics, no silly conversations —'

'Of course you can go, sweetie,' Mrs Bennet said at once, glaring at her husband and turning to Lydia. 'You have fun – but do eat something first.'

'Denny'll buy me something at the bar,' Lydia replied airily.

'Lydia, you can't let him do that – you said he was a

student,' Jane interjected. 'And believe me, students don't have spare cash.'

Lydia pouted and then brightened.

'OK, so can I have my allowance early?' she asked, turning to her mother (past experience having taught her that her terminally uncool father had no idea what it cost to be fifteen). 'And an increase, now that we're rich?'

'You most certainly cannot,' her father expostulated as Alice got up and walked over to the sideboard for her purse. 'It's still only July and it's time you learned that money —'

'Oh sweetheart, you are naughty!' her mother teased, cutting him short. 'But just this once.'

She reached for her purse.

'Right, since my opinions are completely superfluous in this family, I'm taking my meal into my study.' Harry, teeth clenched, stood up and picked up his plate.

'Don't go, Dad,' Lizzie cried, irritated at her mother's total indulgence of Lydia. 'Tell us about Drew. When is he coming?'

'A week tomorrow,' her father said in clipped tones, glancing at his wife as she scrabbled in her bag for her purse. 'So you lot will all have broken up for the summer and can spend time with him.'

He took a gulp of wine, dabbed his mouth and continued enthusiastically, though still refusing to sit down. 'He's over in the UK as part of his hotel management training scheme, which sounds fascinating . . .'

'Not,' muttered Lydia.

'Anyway, he wants to see the sights and watch some

cricket – I thought Toby could take him to a match.'

'Oh.' Lizzie caught Jane's eye and pulled a face.

'Now come on, Elizabeth,' her father said. 'It's hardly going to kill you to part with Toby for one Saturday. You see each other every five minutes and —'

'Not any more, we don't,' Lizzie interrupted. 'We've split up.'

'You have done *what*?'

Lizzie's mother was so distraught that she dropped her purse, spilling coins all over the wood block floor. 'What did you do? How could you have let this happen?'

'What did *I* do?' Lizzie burst out. 'I saw sense, that's what I did. Mum, I'm not even eighteen yet. I don't want to hang out with someone who's already planning how many kids we'll have.'

'Good on you, Lizzie,' her father said.

'But he's like one of the family,' Alice cried, throwing him a murderous look. 'Like the son we never had and you two were perfect for one another. What does the minister say?'

Mrs Bennet always referred to Toby's father by the totally inaccurate job description rather than his name, although whether this was out of snobbery or an inability to keep a straight face while speaking of a man who gloried in the name of Xenophon, Lizzie had never worked out.

'And just what am I supposed to do with this Drew person now,' Mrs Bennet went on, before Lizzie could answer, 'if Toby's not around to keep him out of our hair?'

At this point, her husband, who had been hovering by

the door, slammed his plate back down on the table and glared at her. 'Don't talk like that about the son of my dearest friend,' he retorted. 'Ambrose and I were in business together and —'

'And because you followed some of his damn stupid ideas, you lost a whole load of money,' Alice snapped back, slamming her purse on the table. 'Money that would have paid for our girls to go to private schools and —'

'None of which is Andrew's fault,' Harry retaliated. 'Besides, he doesn't need Toby to entertain him. I shall take a few days off from the office, and anyway, the girls will enjoy taking him out and about.'

'I could take him litter-picking in Rockingham Forest,' Meredith suggested.

'The excitement would probably kill him,' Lydia muttered, her hand outstretched for the twenty-pound note her mother had retrieved from the floor. 'This guy – is he fit?'

'Fit? Well, he's never mentioned any illness,' her father replied.

'Dad! Fit – as in sexy, cute, snoggable.'

Her father sighed. 'I really don't know,' he snapped. 'He did say he was very into Scrabble, though.'

'That,' muttered Lydia, 'is so not a turn on.'

Lizzie was about to take a shower when her mobile phone bleeped.

R u back? Can't w8 2 c u! Life here sucks. Catch up 2moro? Emily xx

Lizzie's fingers hovered over the keys. She was very fond of Emily, but right now she wasn't in the mood to listen to all her problems ('I'll never get a guy, I'm useless, my life's so boring, I'm hideous . . .'). Not that her low self-esteem was all her fault – Emily's parents constantly compared her to her younger sister Maria, who was an A-star-type student and really pretty; Emily, on the other hand, struggled to keep up with work in the Sixth Form and had what her kinder friends called an interesting face and what her father had been heard to label 'plain as a pikestaff'. Lizzie was in the middle of a campaign to give her friend a totally new image, but not tonight.

Before she could key in a reply the phone jangled out the opening bars of the latest Ecstatics hit.

Toby calling.

She closed her eyes, willing the answerphone to cut in. He'd been phoning and texting almost hourly since their row and she knew that she should really talk to him. But what was the point? It wasn't as if he had anything new to say. That was the thing about Toby; he was so predictable.

She knew she couldn't avoid him for ever. A-levels were over, and they'd both officially left school, but like loads of the school-leavers, Toby was getting paid to do sports coaching for the tennis squad most mornings, and Lizzie was helping with rehearsals for the Key Stage 3 end-of-term concert. They were bound to bump into one another. But, she decided, she would deal with that when it happened. For now she'd simply switch off and let him leave a voicemail. It would say exactly the same as all the texts he had bombarded her with: *I love you. I can't live without you. Ring me. I'll do anything.*

And that was the problem. He would do anything. Except the one thing she wanted – simply to be left alone.

Lydia burst into Lizzie's bedroom minutes after she'd switched off her light and settled down to sleep. 'Lizzie, I have to talk to you. If you don't help me out over this one, I'll never speak to you again!'

'For heaven's sake, Lydia, it's half past eleven!'

Dealing with Lydia in drama queen mode was more than she could stand right now.

'Sorry, but this is, like, so crucial,' her sister gabbled. 'You have to help me.'

Lizzie eyed her sister more closely. Her face bore the drying streaks of recent tears and her eyes were suspiciously pink. 'What's wrong?' she asked more gently.

'It's Dad, he's just such a dinosaur. You know what he's done? Grounded me.'

'This wouldn't have something to do with the fact that you went out without permission? Got back late?'

Lydia nodded. 'Ten-thirty is such an unreasonable curfew,' she moaned. 'Amber's allowed out till midnight.'

'Amber's a spoilt brat,' muttered Lizzie. Amber had been Lydia's best friend since primary school; the kind of kid who could wrap her mother round her little finger, usually by threatening to hate whichever new man was on the scene in her mum's life at the time.

'She's not spoilt – she's just got a free-thinking mother.'

'Drop the thinking bit and you could be right,' Lizzie murmured.

'Whatever. Anyway, I've got a plan.'

Lizzie groaned inwardly. In recent years, Lydia's famous plans had landed her in A&E twice, the local police station once, and in detention at school more times than Lizzie could remember.

'If it involves me —' she began.

'It doesn't – well, it does sort of, but only for a tiny minute and . . .'

'Go on.' Lizzie was resigned to hearing her sister out, if only to get rid of her and get some sleep.

'Denny's going to be at the Bingleys' tomorrow evening, right? He's mates with their kids. That's the only reason I've agreed to go to the party in the first place. Thing is, he's planning to get a whole group of guys from the college to go into Meryton later and he's invited me – Amber's going too, cos she, like, so wants to pull Tim. I told you about Tim, yeah – he's the one —'

'Lydia, get to the point.'

'Well, the thing is, I'm going with him of course and —'

'No way is Dad going to fall for that one,' Lizzie observed. 'We were never allowed to go into Meryton on a Saturday night at your age.'

'Stuff that – I'm going to pretend to be ill, you're going to take me home, then I'll slip out of the house, and by the time you get back from the party, it'll be too late for Dad to do anything.' She eyed Lizzie eagerly. 'So what do you say?'

'No.'

'What do you mean, no? You have to – if I don't go,

Denny'll find someone else, and my life will be over.'

'I very much doubt it. Night night, Lydia.'

'You know something, Elizabeth Bennet? You are *so* up yourself!'

As Lydia slammed the door so violently that a crack appeared in the newly painted ceiling, Lizzie felt her eyes prick with tears. It wasn't that she gave a toss for her sister's opinion, it was just that Lydia had used the very same words as Toby had yelled at her twenty-four hours before.

But it wasn't true. She wasn't up herself. She simply saw people as they really were. And if they didn't like it, that was their problem.

CHAPTER 3

'Tease him, laugh at him . . . I dearly love a laugh.'
(Jane Austen, *Pride and Prejudice*)

THE BENNETS WERE AMONG THE LAST TO ARRIVE AT THE party the following evening, largely because Lizzie's mother had spent almost two hours deciding what to wear. The result – a billowing fuchsia-pink skirt that barely skimmed her knees, a sleeveless cotton top trimmed with home-made ribbon roses that would have suited someone half her age and a lilac fascinator – was, Lizzie thought, at best unwise, and at worst disastrous.

'You don't understand,' her mother had declared when Lizzie ventured to suggest she was a tad over-dressed for the occasion. 'We're moving in different circles now. We don't want the Bingleys to think we are new-money upstarts.'

'Which we are,' Lizzie had replied, and then gave her mother's arm a squeeze by way of apology for her unerring honesty. 'I mean, we don't really fit in round here, do we?'

Mrs Bennet sniffed. 'Of course we do! We are simply now living the way we should have been years ago had your father not been taken in by that Ambrose. And by the way, I simply won't have you going to the party in jeans.'

There followed a lengthy argument about clothes, a further delay when Meredith announced that she wasn't going to the party because she was down on the ditch-clearing rota with her Youth for Conservation group and yet more time wasted hanging about for Mr Bennet, who just had to hear the end of his new recording of *La Traviata* before leaving. By the time they reached the wrought-iron gates of Netherfield, Mrs Bennet's face was almost the same colour as her outfit and her agitation levels were through the roof.

'Wow! That's some house!' Lizzie gasped.

Even Lydia, with all her pretensions towards sophistication, was rendered almost speechless at the sight of the Bingleys' home. Standing in several acres on the edge of the village, backing on to open countryside a quarter of a mile from Priory Park, Netherfield Manor was an imposing three-storey Georgian house with lofty chimneys, sash windows and swathes of clematis and Virginia creeper clambering up the walls. Worn stone steps led up to a porticoed front door, and either side of the sweeping gravel drive were manicured lawns flanked by larch and willow trees. To one side of the house, a wrought-iron gate was wedged open with a croquet mallet to which was attached a luminous pink card in the shape of an arrow bearing the words *LOAM Party this way*.

'What on earth does *Loam* mean?' Lizzie muttered, as they followed their mother, who was eagerly dragging her husband along the path at the side of the house.

'Some quaint village custom, perhaps?' teased Jane. 'Maybe there's going to be cheese rolling and dung throwing!'

'It's all a bit posh, isn't it?' Lizzie remarked, eyeing the huge expanse of lawn, the pond complete with fountain, the walled vegetable garden and the distant shimmering of a swimming pool. 'Very *Homes and Gardens*.'

Their mother turned round, flapping a hand anxiously at them. 'Be quiet, behave,' she urged, fiddling with one of her pearl earrings, a sign Lizzie recognised as showing just how nervous she was under all her bravado. 'Now girls, you will – well, make a good impression, won't you? If we're going to be bosom buddies . . . Oh look! Here comes Vanessa.'

Mrs Bingley, wearing a simple but very chic lilac linen dress and a straw sunhat, hurried up to them, hand outstretched. 'Alice, you're here. And . . .' She paused, her eyes resting on Alice's attire and then swiftly recovered herself. 'And your girls – lovely.'

She fanned herself with a hand bedecked with several large diamond and amethyst rings. 'This heat – I've never known a July like it,' she said. 'Now do come and have a cooling drink, all of you.'

She led the family across the lawn, past the clusters of guests clutching glasses and balancing plates, towards the vast terrace, on which a trestle table was laid out with jugs of Pimm's and dishes piled with crudités and upmarket-looking canapés.

Suddenly, Lydia let out a screech of delight.

'Denny! Babe!' Without a backward glance, she dashed across the lawn, almost colliding with a stout man in shorts that lacked any kind of sartorial elegance, and straight into Denny's arms.

'Good heavens!' Mrs Bingley was clearly taken aback. 'Don't tell me your daughter is – er – well, a friend of Denis?'

'She's so popular, bless her, with all the boys,' Lizzie's mum laughed. 'I can't keep track of them all.'

'Well, he's one I'd keep track of if she was my child,' Vanessa said, gesturing to them to help themselves to drinks. 'Used to be such a nice little kid too . . . my two played with him, rode ponies together and then somehow he got in with quite the wrong . . . anyway, that's your business. What I need to do is fill you in on all this ghastly business that's blighting our village. This isn't just any party – it's a party with a purpose.'

She eyed the obviously bewildered group.

'LOAM – you'll have read about our campaign, of course?'

'Er, well, no . . . I,' Mrs Bennet stammered.

'Longbourn Oaks Against Masts,' Vanessa stressed. 'They're planning to put a phone mast in our village. On the church tower, no less. Outrageous!'

She gestured in the direction of St Peter's Church, the tower of which could be seen through the trees at the side of the house.

'Happens a lot these days,' said Lizzie's father. 'Sign of the times.'

'Maybe, but that doesn't make it right,' Mrs Bingley insisted. 'It's totally inappropriate. I told the vicar he should be ashamed of himself. Desecrating the house of God.' She turned to Alice. 'I'm sure you agree?'

'Oh definitely, absolutely, yes indeed,' Alice gabbled.

'Good thing, I say,' Harry observed. 'Might mean we get a decent signal round here. I have to go halfway down the garden to make a call. Damn nuisance.'

'You don't mean to say – but the view from our upstairs windows – it'll be ruined,' Vanessa protested. 'I'm writing to the bishop, of course.'

'The bishop?' Harry remarked. 'Well, of course, I'm sure he'll see your point of view. The view being ruined – terrible thing. Far worse than desecrating the house of God, then?'

Vanessa blushed as Jane and Lizzie exchanged amused glances.

'What I meant was – that is, the —'

'Harry will have his little joke,' Lizzie's mum butted in, applying the heel of her sandal to Harry's instep.

'Oh, I see – you're winding me up!' Vanessa fluttered her eyelashes at him. This was no mean achievement considering the amount of mascara weighing them down. 'Naughty man!' She smiled girlishly at Harry, who suddenly found a neighbouring rose bush to be of huge interest.

'Well now,' Vanessa went on, 'why don't I find my crew and let the young people sort themselves out while we get down to business.' She glanced around the garden. 'Ah, there they are!' She pointed to a group of kids at the far side of the lawn by the swimming pool. 'Charlie! Caroline!'

A tall, well-built girl with an auburn bob and a large chest bulging somewhat provocatively from a jade green sundress nudged one of the guys and they broke away from their group and ambled towards them. In the short time it took to reach them, the girl had scanned them all from top to toe and back again and, judging by the thinly veiled sneer on her heavily glossed lips, she wasn't much impressed by what she saw.

'Darlings, these are the Bennets,' Mrs Bingley announced. 'They're new to the village – well, I say village. Actually, they're in Priory Park.'

From her tone, Lizzie judged that no amount of estate agent hype could convince Mrs Bingley that the new development was anything other than an intrusion into their tight-knit community.

'Cool,' her son said cheerfully, grinning at them.

Caroline merely grunted.

'Now, why don't you get to know one another while I take Alice and Harry away and bring them up to speed about what's going on,' their mother ordered, gesturing to Lizzie's parents to follow her over to the terrace. 'You'll need the information pack and I've drawn up a list of the help we need before the planning meeting and then there's . . .'

Her voice faded as she ushered them away.

'Is there anything worse than a campaigning parent?' Charlie – slim, sandy-haired and with the sort of boyish grin that suggested he had never quite left the *Just William* stage behind – raised an eyebrow at his mother's retreating back. 'Honestly, I don't know why she bothers – it's not like it's going make a bit of difference.'

'That's typical of you,' his sister remarked scathingly, nibbling on a curl of smoked salmon. 'Sit back and let the world trample all over you.'

'I just think,' Charlie said, 'that it's a bit rich when people who spend half their lives glued to their mobile phones then moan like crazy when someone wants to erect a mast.'

'They don't have to put it where it's going to ruin our view, though, do they?' Caroline cut in.

'Oh, so if they stuck it in the middle of an estate full of social housing, it would be OK, would it?' Lizzie suggested dryly, irritated at being ignored.

'Lizzie,' Jane whispered urgently. 'Shh.'

'Sorry, but surely that's not what matters?' Lizzie went on, only half aware that it was her pent-up irritations with Toby that were driving her to be so outspoken with strangers. 'The church is right next to the village school. What about all that radiation?'

'You sound like Meredith,' Jane teased and then turned hastily to Charlie. 'That's our other sister, she's not here but she's very hot on environmental issues and —'

'Don't tell me there're more of you,' Caroline gasped. 'What happened? Did your parents keep trying in hopes of a boy?'

'Caro!' Charlie snapped. 'You are something else, you know that.'

'So-reee, it was only a joke.'

'What's going on? Don't tell me you two are bickering again?' A broad-shouldered guy with deep-set, charcoal-grey eyes sauntered up to them, tossing a croquet ball from one hand to the other.

Charlie grinned. 'I've just been firmly put in my place by . . .' He turned to Lizzie. 'Oh – I don't even know your name.'

'Lizzie,' said Lizzie. 'And this is Jane and over there, that's Lydia and Katie.'

She pointed across to the lower lawn where Katie was making a valiant attempt to tag along with Lydia and a couple of guys who were bashing croquet balls through hoops and giggling hysterically.

'And this,' Charlie announced, gesturing to his friend, 'is James Darcy, who on a good day is my best mate and on a bad day, a pain in the butt.'

He punched his friend teasingly in the ribs. To Lizzie's amusement, Caroline had suddenly discarded her supercilious expression and was sidling closer to this newcomer, her sharp features softened by what Lizzie assumed was an attempt at an alluring pout.

James glanced at Lizzie and Jane and gave a brief nod. Lizzie thought that if he could manage to force a smile, he would be quite cute; his finely chiselled features were softened by dark hair that flopped over his right eye and he had just enough of a five o'clock shadow to be appealing, without looking scruffy. It was, in fact, a look that Lizzie, so used to the chubby-cheeked, blue-eyed and over-clean Toby, had started to favour of late.

'James is in a sulk,' Charlie said grinning. 'Staying with us is a bit downmarket for him – he usually spends the summer living it up at the family chateau in France.'

'Leave it out, Charlie,' James retorted. 'I'm not sulking, just bored stiff. Look, why don't we —'

His words were interrupted by the jangling of a bell from the terrace, and judging by the thunderous look James flung in Charlie's direction, it was just as well.

'Over here, everyone, please!' Mrs Bingley's strident tones reminded Lizzie of her primary school headmistress, whose voice at playtime could be heard above a force-ten gale.

'This is where it could start to get embarrassing,' Charlie sighed, as the guests began obediently moving towards the rows of chairs set on the patio. 'This was meant to be a thank-you party for everyone who rallied round when Pa got ill; trust Mum to turn it into a full-blown protest!'

'Your father's been ill?' Jane asked. 'I'm sorry.'

'Yes, he had some sort of —'

'For God's sake, Charlie, you don't have to share all our private business with a load of strangers!' Caroline snapped. 'He was ill and he's getting better, OK? That's all you need to know.'

'Sorry, I didn't mean to intrude,' Jane flushed scarlet.

'Caro, for God's sake,' Charlie hissed, and turned to the girls, his voice artificially bright. 'Come on, meet the rest of the gang – we were just debating what to do for the rest of the evening while Ma and her cronies put the world to rights.'

He led them across the lawn and down to the swimming pool, where a group of kids were hanging out round a trestle table under a flapping awning. As they drew nearer, Lizzie gasped in surprise.

'Hey, Emily!'

At the sound of Lizzie's voice, a plump, freckle-faced girl with strands of caramel-coloured hair escaping from a ponytail spun round, her face breaking into a grin.

'Liz!' She ran forward and gave Lizzie a hug. 'I didn't

know you'd be here – this is so cool! I've missed you. And I've been texting and calling you non-stop all day. I thought you must have missed your flight.'

'I've had the phone switched off,' Lizzie told her, not wanting to confess that she'd been putting off replying to her friend's text all day. 'And our landline's not working yet.'

'You? Switched off – Miss Communicator herself?' Emily teased. 'That has to be a first. How come?'

'Later.'

One look at Lizzie's face and Emily's expression changed to one of concern.

'Are you OK?' she whispered, edging closer to Lizzie, who was staring into the middle distance.

'Never better – not. So what are you doing here anyway? You never said you knew this crowd.'

'Oh yes, known them for ages. Dad and Mr B were churchwardens together, back before he got ill, and Mum plays tennis with Vanessa,' Emily explained. 'That's why Mum's doing the catering at a discount for her.'

Emily's mother had started ChicChefs the year before with a couple of friends because, as she explained to Lizzie's mum, despite not needing the money (the Lucases were loaded) she needed breathing space now that her husband had retired and was under her feet all day.

'I'm supposed to be helping,' Emily admitted, 'but I dropped two trays of food and spilled a jug of Pimm's on the vicar.'

Lizzie laughed. 'So no change there, then,' she said.

When it came to manual dexterity, Emily was a non-starter.

'Hey, so you two know each other, yeah?' Charlie asked, scooping ice cubes into highball glasses.

'Sure – we are at the same school,' Emily told him, squeezing Lizzie's arm. 'Well, officially we've just left, actually.'

'Where's that, then?' James turned and glanced at Lizzie enquiringly. 'Clearly not Benenden, since you don't know Caroline, but your face is familiar. You're not at Roedean, are you?'

Lizzie burst out laughing at the idea of her father forking out thousands for a private school education for five children.

'Hardly!' she replied. 'Meryton Academy.'

'Academy? You mean a state school? A comprehensive?' James's dark eyebrows shot skywards. 'Really?'

There was something in his tone of voice that irritated Lizzie beyond belief.

'And what's wrong with a state school?' she demanded, accepting a glass of Pimm's from Charlie, who was desperately trying to catch James's eye.

'You want a list?' James asked. 'Dumbed-down teaching, sports fields sold off for supermarkets, sod all discipline . . .'

'And the rest,' murmured Caroline.

'That is so prejudiced!' Lizzie bristled, glancing at Emily in the hope that she would back her up. 'Meryton Ack's way up the league tables and —'

'Like that means anything,' James retorted.

'Cool it, James, yeah?' Charlie's tone had lost its usual

banter as he glared at his friend.

'I was only pointing out . . .'

'Well, don't.'

What could have been an uneasy silence was broken by Katie tearing up to Lizzie and grabbing her arm. 'You won't believe what Lydia's done,' she said. 'Only gone into Meryton and not even asked me along.'

'Gone? I just saw her a minute ago.' Lizzie frowned.

'Well, she's not here now. She went off with Denny, on his motorbike, just a moment ago.' Katie told her, her face paler than ever. 'They're going to a club.'

'Clickers, I bet,' Emily cut in eagerly. 'Lydia said that Tim and Amber were texting everyone to say they've pitched up there, and it's two-for-one night on drinks and what's more, Capital Caterpillar are playing.'

'I don't believe it!' Lizzie exploded, grabbing her mobile phone from the pocket of her jeans and calling Lydia. 'Dad will go spare.'

'Has she told Mum?' Jane asked at the same moment.

'Get real,' Katie replied scornfully. 'Like she's really gonna do that.' She turned to Lizzie. 'And she's hardly going to answer the phone, is she?' she reasoned. 'You're wasting your time.'

'Well, if you ask me . . . Katie, where are you going?' Lizzie called, but Katie had dashed off round the side of the house.

'Seems to me like they've got the right idea,' James muttered, glancing across the lawn to where the guests were still listening to Mrs Bingley's urgent appeals for what she called active protest. 'Beats hanging around here.'

'Great,' Charlie pronounced. 'So what are we waiting for?'

He turned to Jane. 'You're up for it, yeah? I haven't had a drink – I can take Ma's car. We won't all get into mine.'

'Well, I don't know.'

'Go on, it'll be a laugh,' he urged. 'Unless of course – I mean, you may have other things to do?'

'No, nothing,' Jane assured him. 'OK then, that'd be good.'

Lizzie stared at her sister in amazement. It usually took Jane, who had made shyness into an art form, weeks to feel at ease with new people (when she went to uni she had spent the first ten days phoning home in tears every few hours) and here she was proposing to go clubbing with perfect strangers.

'I'll come in your car,' Caroline said, sidling up to James. 'But we'll need to get back early – I've got to be up at six to get Gigi ready for a dressage lesson.'

'You ride?' Jane gasped, her eyes lighting up. 'Have you got your own horse?'

'We've got three,' Charlie said. 'Well, one's only a pony, really, but we can't bear to part with him! We keep them over at the College. British Horse Society students get to ride them and we get reduced fees. Why? Are you keen too?'

'I love it,' Jane enthused. 'I went every week when I was a kid, but then it got too expensive.'

'Hear that, Caro?' Charlie exclaimed.' Jane could take Nutmeg out some time. She could do with being ridden again.'

To Lizzie's surprise, Caroline smiled broadly at Jane.

'Sure,' she said. 'Any time you like – be good to have someone to help out.'

'Yoo hoo, girls!' Lizzie, who had been on the point of trying Lydia's phone again, froze in horror as her mother came tripping across the lawn to them. 'Having fun? I think I'm a bit squiffy what with all the Pimm's – you don't realise how much you're drinking, do you, until . . .'

James and Caroline made no attempt to suppress their titters as Mrs Bennet wobbled and grabbed hold of the table.

'So you've made lots of friends, cherubs?' she went on, beaming at her daughters. 'Ever so stylish here, isn't it? And I've been given a job to do on the mokity . . . committee – for the toepress . . . protest.'

'Is she for real, or some extra from a downmarket soap?' James's whispered remark to Caroline was clear enough for Lizzie to hear. 'And what's with the hat?'

'Mum, I need to talk to you.' Lizzie grabbed her mother's arm and piloted her away from the group.

'You're drunk,' she muttered accusingly. 'You know you can't take more than one glass at the best of times. What were you thinking of?'

'Don't be zilly, Lissie,' her mother retorted. 'I'm as sober as a – as a —'

'Whatever,' Lizzie interrupted. 'The thing is, about Lydia. She's —'

'She's coming out with us for a bit, OK, Mum?' Jane cut in throwing Lizzie a warning glance. 'We're going to Meryton with Charlie.'

'He's a bit of all right, isn't he?' Jane winced as her

mother's voice rang round the garden. 'Nice bum. If I was thirty years younger . . .'

Alice giggled and then hiccupped loudly as Mr Bennet appeared at her side.

'I think you and I should be making tracks,' he remarked, taking his wife's arm and looking apologetically over his shoulder at a group of astounded guests.

'Dad?'

'Later, Lizzie,' her father replied. 'I think getting your mother home and into a horizontal position is the most important thing right now.'

Lizzie supposed she should be grateful that her mother's inebriation had diverted her father's attention away from the fact that Lydia was nowhere to be seen. But watching her parents make their way across the garden, with the eyes of several guests firmly fixed on her mother's tottering progress, Lizzie had an overwhelming desire to curl up and die.

'Why on earth did you cover up for Lydia?' she muttered to Jane, as they followed the others to the front of the house. Now Katie'll want to hang out with us.'

'She won't,' Jane said, gesturing towards the front gate. 'She's just been sick. In the flower bed.'

'Oh no,' Lizzie groaned. 'What is it with this family?'

'Don't worry, no one's noticed – well, not yet,' Jane smiled. 'I'll go and sort her – tell her to go home.'

'Which we could do too? You're not really up for clubbing, are you?'

'It might be fun,' Jane said, avoiding Lizzie's gaze. 'I mean, you're always telling me to get a life and forget – well, the past. And anyway, we ought to make sure

Lyddy's OK, right? But I'm only going if you'll come.'

Jane's eyes darted from her sister to Charlie and back again.

'Please.' 'OK,' Lizzie smiled. 'Since you insist. But not for long. This lot get right up my nose.'

CHAPTER 4

'My good opinion once lost is lost forever.'
(Jane Austen, *Pride and Prejudice*)

SET IN ONE OF THE TOWN'S NOW DEFUNCT SHOE factories, Clickers was Meryton's newest and classiest night spot, although as James remarked dryly, given the standard set by the rest of the clubs, that was hardly a glowing recommendation. The instant they arrived, he ambled over to the bar looking, if anything, more uptight than ever.

As soon as her eyes had adjusted to the dim light, Lizzie scanned the room in search of Lydia.

'Hey, come and dance!' Charlie appeared and seized Jane's hand. 'I've told James to get the drinks in, but there's a hell of a queue – so come on!' And with that, he dragged her off towards the spiral staircase that led to the mezzanine floor.

'This place is so cool,' Emily enthused, bopping rather unrhythmically to the music. 'Hey, do you think that guy over there is on his own? As in available?'

She jerked her head in the direction of a long-haired, lanky guy in torn jeans, who was leaning against the bar and staring disconsolately into a pint of lager.

'Emily, he's disgusting.' Lizzie pulled a face. 'He looks like he hasn't washed in a week. What are you on?'

Emily shrugged. 'He's male, he's on his own and if he can avoid the entry fee to this place, he's got cash,' she replied. 'And besides, I quite go for the grunge look.'

'Well, you can do better than him,' Lizzie assured her, pushing past more dancers and heading for a group of girls giggling in the far corner of the club.

'That's easy for you to say, since your love life is totally sorted,' her friend snapped. 'You've got it made – looks, brain, figure. People like me can't afford to be fussy.'

'Oh, don't start the whole self-pity routine again, Emily, for God's sake,' Lizzie snapped. 'If you made a bit more effort to . . .'

'To what? Go on, say it – to be more like you, right?' To Lizzie's horror, Emily burst into tears.

'Em, I'm sorry, honestly, I didn't mean that, no way.' She touched her friend's arm, feeling a complete idiot for being so thoughtless.

'I'm just in a mood – what you said – well, the point is, Toby and me – we've split. So you see, I'm not sorted. Well, I am but . . .' Emily stopped mid sob. 'Split? You and Toby? I don't believe it.' She stared at Lizzie in amazement. 'How dare he dump you? I would never have thought that of him.'

'Emily, *I* dumped him,' Lizzie confessed.

'Are you *totally mad*? So – have you found someone else?'

'Get real,' Lizzie retorted. 'Right now, I want another relationship like I want a hole in the head.'

'So – Toby's, like, available?' Emily brightened visibly.

'I guess he is,' Lizzie said smiling.

'Great,' Emily replied. 'I'll invite him.'

'To what?'

'My eighteenth, silly,' Emily said. 'You put it in your diary.'

'Oh. Yes. But —'

'It's OK for you,' Emily cut in quickly. 'You'll have loads of guys fawning after you. And it is my party and I'm short on available guys and if Toby comes I could . . .'

'Sure. Great idea,' Lizzie said, knowing full well that by the day of the party, Toby would be sailing in Greece, but judging it best to say nothing. 'Now can we please drop the subject and find my sister?'

'You look for her,' Emily said. 'I need the loo. Oh, and text me Toby's phone number, yeah?'

'Emily Lucas, you are something else.' Lizzie turned and headed up the spiral staircase. She spotted Amber, skirt hitched up round her thighs as she perched on the knee of a boy with wildly curly black hair and a glazed expression; and at the other end of the room, surrounded by a group of admiring guys, she found her sister, dancing to the beat of a live band with all the flair of a finalist on *Strictly Come Dancing*. Watching her as she punched the air, wiggled her hips and pouted seductively at one guy after another, Lizzie was torn between envy of her confidence and sheer joy in life, and alarm at the signals she was sending out. Looking the way she did, it was no wonder that the bouncers hadn't challenged her for ID on the way in.

'Lydia!'

Her sister caught sight of her, grinned and sashayed across, dragging Denny and another guy with her.

'Hiya,' she said cheerfully. 'So you came. Isn't this the coolest place? This is Zak, by the way. Who's here? Jane? That Charlie guy?'

'You are so going to be in trouble when you get home,' Lizzie said, ignoring her question. 'Dad'll go ballistic.'

'Sure he will,' Lydia said laughing. 'But he won't do anything. Well, he might ground me.'

She turned to Denny and giggled. 'But that's never stopped me yet. And anyway, I've had my fun – they can't take that away from me, can they?' With that, she seized Denny's hand. 'Come on, buy me a drink – I'm gasping!'

Watching them clatter down the staircase, followed by the rest of the crowd, Lizzie felt a fool. She was nearly eighteen, for heaven's sake – she should be partying, not worrying about her sister who was, after all, more than capable of looking after herself.

She ran back down the stairs, catching the strains of her favourite Purple Panic hit being played during the band break. As she reached the bottom and the music died away, she heard her name.

'Me? With Lizzie Bennet? For God's sake, Charlie, you have to be joking!' The clipped tones were unmistakably James's.

Lizzie took two steps back as softly as she could, sat down on the stairs and strained to catch what they were saying.

'What's wrong with her?' Charlie asked. 'OK, she's not as stunning as Jane – Jane's totally gorgeous but . . .'

'Charlie, you think any girl who so much as smiles at you is gorgeous,' James remarked. 'OK, I agree Jane's pretty in a twee, Disney princess kind of way. But Lizzie? Why would I want to spend time with her?'

'I want to take Jane on somewhere, and you know, get to know her a bit better,' Lizzie heard Charlie say slightly self-consciously. 'And we can hardly dump Lizzie.'

'Like that's my problem?' James said. 'Come off it, Charlie – I told you I've come here to chill out – it's been a bloody awful year.'

'Exactly! But you have to move on, get a life.'

'And I'm going to do that by spending my time with some lippy schoolgirl with an inflated opinion of herself – not to mention the mother from hell.'

'I'm not asking you to entertain the mother, am I?' Charlie retaliated. 'And anyway, if anyone was lippy, it was you. The way you went on about state schools, you sounded a right snob.'

'It was Lizzie who went off on one about how bloody marvellous that academy place was,' James said. 'Like I hardly think so. And God, that sister of theirs! Slag of the Century or what?'

'You know what? I'm tired of the way you're always finding fault with everything and everyone.'

'I just happen to live in the real world and see things as they are,' James retorted. 'It's called being an adult.'

Charlie sighed and shook his head. 'It's called looking on the black side of everything,' he muttered, 'but suit yourself – I'm going to ask Jane anyway and if Lizzie —'

At that moment, as Lizzie was forced to shift her

position to let a couple of girls edge past her, Charlie caught her eye. 'Lizzie!' His cheeks flamed scarlet and he looked as if he wanted the ground to open and swallow him whole. For a moment, as she leaped to her feet, Lizzie felt sorry for him, but then, as James turned to face her, the sneer still on his lips, she decided that if Charlie was stupid enough to associate with a stuck-up guy like James, that was his problem. 'Jane's just gone to the loo and then we're . . . oh! Here she comes.'

The relief on his face was palpable.

'Lizzie, what's up?' Jane had always been able to sense when her sister was angry or upset without the need for words.

'I'm leaving,' Lizzie said.

'Leaving?' Charlie burst out. 'But there's no need . . . I mean, perhaps we could go for a pizza?'

'Oh, please!' Lizzie snapped. 'I would hate to inflict myself on your friend.'

She glared at James. 'Just think how mortified he'd be to have to pass another hour in the company of a lippy state-school kid!'

She pushed past them towards a corner table where Amber and Lydia were shrieking with laughter and twirling paper cocktail umbrellas over Tim and Denny's heads.

'Two choices,' Lizzie snapped at her. 'Come home now and I try to cover for you, or stay here and face the music on your own!'

'God, what's with the grumpy big sister routine?' Amber sniggered. 'You were right, Lyds, she so, like, needs to get a life!'

'Lydia, for the last time,' Lizzie began, but before she could finish, Jane was at her side.

'What's going on? Don't go – Charlie says —'

'I don't care what Charlie says,' Lizzie retorted, dragging her to one side. Then, catching the pained expression on Jane's face, she flashed her a wry smile. 'He's nice – he really is – but his choice of friends . . . do you know what James called me?'

'What?'

'He said . . . Oh, never mind. I'll tell you later. Look, I don't want to spoil your evening. I can get a cab.'

In all honesty, Lizzie was feeling a bit of an idiot. Why hadn't she just ignored James, or better still, challenged him to his face, there and then? Made him realise what a rude, swollen-headed idiot he was? Why hadn't she . . .?

'Charlie says that if you just hang on a bit longer, he'll take us all home.' Jane touched her shoulder and eyed her anxiously. 'Lydia too, OK?'

'And James? I have to share the car with him?'

'Lizzie!'

'OK, OK,' Lizzie held up her hands in surrender. 'But just don't expect me to speak, all right? If I never say another word to that guy as long as I live, it'll be too soon.'

'Well, yes, I agree, that was a pretty awful thing to say,' Jane conceded, after Lizzie had plonked herself down on her sister's bed two hours later and ranted on unceasingly for ten minutes. 'But honestly, don't judge him too harshly. Charlie mentioned to me that James has had a really tough couple of years.'

'Oh right, so he thinks it's OK to inflict his misery on the rest of us,' Lizzie replied. 'And slag us all off.'

'Well, you have to admit . . .'

'I know, I know,' Lizzie sighed. 'Mum made an ass of herself and Lydia was, well, Lydia. But no way am I lippy. I just think for myself. And unlike James I-am-up-myself Darcy, I don't build my whole life on outmoded, upper-class prejudices!'

Jane laughed. 'Why don't you just forget it and go to bed?' she suggested. 'If it bothers you that much, don't give it the air time.'

'Too right,' Lizzie nodded. 'I'm sure he's not losing sleep over his bad manners, so why should I? Besides, I can see you want to be left to dream sweet dreams about Charlie.'

Laughing, she dodged the pillow that her sister hurled at her, and went to bed.

Had she been able to overhear the conversation taking place at that moment in the kitchen at Netherfield, where Caroline, James and Charlie were clearing up the leftovers from the outsize fridge, she might not have slept so easily.

'You do realise,' Charlie was saying, glaring at James, 'that the only reason the evening got cut short was because Lizzie heard your outburst? So thanks – thanks a million.'

'Look, all I'm saying is that the Bennets simply aren't our type. It's obvious; they're clearly new money, they have no class and can you imagine them mixing with our set? I don't think so.'

'Absolutely,' Caroline cut in, scooping salmon pâté on to a cracker. 'I mean, Jane is quite sweet, I guess, but Lizzie . . . Charlie, how could you even think she was the type James would go for?'

'I'm not asking him to have a relationship with her, for God's sake – just to be civil. I think the Bennets are an OK crowd and just because they haven't had the privileges we've had, doesn't make them inferior.'

'You've been with Jane for five hours max,' James reasoned. 'You're always doing this – you meet a girl and your brain ceases to function.'

'Come off it.'

'OK, how about a bet, then?' James said, a grin on his face. 'Let's say I was wrong. I admit, maybe, I should have kept my thoughts to myself, but I'm not like that.'

'You can say that again,' Charlie muttered.

'So, I'll shut up for – oh, let's say the next three weeks, till I leave, right? I bet you a hundred pounds that by then, you'll have seen sense and dropped Jane like a dish of hot cakes, just like you did with Claudia and Pandora.'

'Claudia cheated on me, and Pandora turned out to be gay,' Charlie retorted.

'OK, then, you're on. You stop being so mouthy and bolshie with the Bennets and if you're right, and Jane isn't what she seems, I'll pay up. Deal?'

'Deal!' James smacked palms with Charlie. 'I do so love easy money.'

For Meredith and the twins there was another full week of the summer term left. Lizzie was tied up, not only with helping out at school, but with rehearsals for a wind band concert with the East Midlands Youth Orchestra and her Grade 8 singing exam. But for Jane, at the end of her first year at London University, the summer vacation had already started. Which was why, finding her sister already chomping her way through a bowl of muesli at half past seven on Monday morning, Lizzie was somewhat startled.

'What are you doing up?' she asked, as she polished her French horn. 'On Friday, you said you wanted long lazy lie-ins all week.'

'Yes, well, that was then,' Jane murmured, avoiding Lizzie's gaze. 'Thing is, I got a text from Caroline last night. She's invited me over to ride. And Charlie . . .'

She paused, giving Lizzie a sidelong glance.

'Well, he might be around,' she finished, colouring slightly. 'He's really nice, don't you think? Sort of sensible and yet . . .'

'Nice, definitely. Sensible? I don't think so,' her sister replied. 'At least not when it comes to his choice of friends. That arrogant sod James.'

'Oh, Lizzie, you're not still going on about him, surely,' Jane teased. 'You're always like this – talk about a dog with a bone! Anyway, if Charlie likes him, he can't be that bad.'

'Janey, I know that you love the entire universe and would make excuses for Osama bin Laden if it came to it, but that guy!'

Lizzie opened the fridge and grabbed a pot of yoghurt. 'Anyway, don't let's waste our breath on James Darcy. What about you and Charlie? I mean . . .'

'Don't start getting ideas,' Jane said laughing. 'He's

just a nice guy who happens to have a sister with horses. Thank goodness I didn't chuck out my jodhpurs – they're a bit on the tight side, but they'll do.' She glanced at the kitchen clock. 'I'd better get going,' she said. 'Caroline said I needed to be there for eight. Don't you think it's great of her to ask me?'

'Mmm.'

'What do you mean, mmm?' Jane demanded, putting her cereal bowl into the dishwasher and taking a last gulp of juice.

'Oh, nothing,' Lizzie sighed. 'It's just that – well, she's ever so stuck-up, don't you think? You know, public school and all that. Don't you find it a bit – I don't know – over the top?'

'No, I don't,' Jane said. 'If anyone was over the top, it was Mum. And Lydia.'

'Don't remind me,' Lizzie groaned. 'You'd have thought Mum would lie low after making such a fool of herself at the party, but the way she carried on at church yesterday . . .'

'I guess she's so used to being in the midst of things at St Peter's that she wanted to make her mark at this new place,' Jane reasoned. 'And be fair – she was only singing your praises as a soprano and trying to whip up support for this phone mast campaign.'

She ran a finger gingerly round the tight waistband of her jodhpurs and undid the top button. 'What's more, over coffee she came up with the idea that they should focus the campaign on how close the mast will be to the primary school,' Jane added. 'Which for her was pretty spot on.'

'She got that from me,' Lizzie smiled. 'But yes, good on her for stating the obvious. I just wish she could do things more quietly and not in full view of people like James.'

'I thought you didn't want to mention his name again,' Jane commented. 'Does it matter what he thinks?'

Lizzie opened her mouth to answer and then thought better of it. Of course it didn't matter at all. Why should the opinions of the most insufferable guy she'd ever had the misfortune to meet be of any concern to her?

By Thursday morning, it seemed to Lizzie that every member of her family was having a less stressful week than she was. The rehearsals weren't going that well and her nerves were beginning to kick in for her singing exam. She had to do well – really well; unbeknown to anyone else, so much depended on her getting Distinction. She hadn't even shared her plans with Jane, because verbalising them might be bad luck.

Emily was insisting on showing up at school every day, ostensibly to assist with costumes and make helpful comments, but in reality because Toby was coaching on the all-weather courts and she liked watching his thighs from the window of the music suite. Lizzie didn't want Toby – but she didn't want to hear about his wonderful muscles and sexy backside every ten minutes either.

Katie and Lydia were on a geography field trip to the Brecon Beacons. Katie had sent eight texts full of angst about spiders, boil-in-the-bag rations and Lydia's escapades with Guy Henson, and Lydia hadn't sent any, presumably on account of being too busy with Guy Henson.

Meredith, basking smugly in the glory of being named Eco Student of the Year for instigating the school's Bat and Bird Box project, had been interviewed by the local paper and Radio Meryton and was set on a career as what she called an eco journalist. She'd even offered to send the *Meryton Chronicle* a daily blog from her forthcoming Wildlife and Wetlands holiday with Youth for Conservation in the Fens.

Mrs Bennet was occupied creating posters for the mast protest, and Lizzie's father was working late every night in order to take time off when Drew arrived and then unwinding by playing *The Ring Cycle* on his new surround sound system at full volume, making it impossible for Lizzie to practise her horn concerto.

And to make things worse, the letter that Lizzie was so desperate to receive still hadn't come.

Jane, far from chilling out, had been over to the stables three times, although Lizzie was somewhat suspicious of Caroline's motives. Her sister confessed to having ridden only once, the rest of her visits being spent cleaning tack, mucking out and shifting dung while, to use Jane's own words, Caroline 'drooled over James and recounted how she'd pulled loads of guys in her time, but none as fit and sexy as JD.'

'God, doesn't that girl make you want to vomit?' Lizzie said that morning, as she hung about in the kitchen waiting for a lift from her father, who was downing his second cup of coffee and flicking through his latest CD catalogue.

'She's nice when you get to know her – it must be pretty dire being at a girls' boarding school all term. And she obviously fancies James like crazy – remember what you used to be like with Toby.'

'Point taken,' Lizzie said, pulling a face. 'And if you enjoy going over there . . .?'

'It's cool,' Jane assured her. 'I'm getting used to being round horses again. And the best bit is that —'

What the best bit was Lizzie didn't discover as at that moment her mother burst into the room. 'It's come, it's come,' she cried. 'Jane, move my car, there's a dear – the lorry can't get up the drive.'

'What's come?' Lizzie asked.

'The new furniture, of course,' her mother declared. 'For the guest bedroom.'

'But we've got furniture.'

'What? That old stuff your grandmother left behind?' her mother retorted. 'Don't be ridiculous – in our position? Vanessa has this wonderful sleigh bed in her guest bedroom.'

'How do you know?' Jane asked.

'Oh, come on, Jane.' Her father smiled, putting his coffee mug into the dishwasher. 'Your mother made it her business to inspect the entire house while we were there last weekend. First, she needed the bathroom so urgently that she simply had to go upstairs; then she left her handbag on the landing and then – which I admit was creative even for her – she decided she needed to see for herself how the phone mast would ruin the view from the Bingleys' bedroom. Subtle, eh?'

He winked at Lizzie. 'Next thing I know she's been to

Parsonson's and ordered the exact replica of Vanessa's furniture.'

'Hers is white; mine's Parisian Cream,' Alice interrupted. 'The man in the shop said white is very last year. Mine was featured in the *Sunday Times*.'

She paused, clearly waiting for a reaction. When none was forthcoming, she glared at Harry.

'The downside,' she declared, 'is that this Drew boy will be the first to use it.'

She sniffed as the letterbox rattled furiously. 'Quickly, get a move on, Jane!'

As Jane obediently grabbed the car keys from the hook above the kitchen table and disappeared into the hall, her mother hot on her heels, her father sank down on to the nearest chair and sighed.

'Do you think you and Jane could hold the fort for a night or so, Lizzie?' he asked. 'Right now, your mum's refusing to come to Heathrow on Saturday morning to meet Drew. Says it awakens cruel memories, which, frankly, is a bit over the top.'

Lizzie smiled, but said nothing.

'I thought perhaps, if I was to book a nice hotel for tomorrow night, get tickets for that musical she wants to see . . .'

'It would get Mum in a good mood,' Lizzie finished with a grin. ''Course we can cope, Dad.'

'You're sure, now? I mean, the twins aren't due back till Saturday morning and Jane'll pick them up if we're not around, and Meredith's —'

'Dad! It's no problem. Have fun. Think about it, what can possibly happen in the next forty-eight hours?'

* * *

'Janey, can you do me a huge favour?' Lizzie asked on Friday morning, while their parents were upstairs arguing about the vast amount of luggage Mrs Bennet thought necessary for a night in London. 'Drop me at school? It's our last rehearsal and I've missed the bus.'

Jane's face fell. 'Oh. Well, I . . . I mean . . . the thing is, we're going riding.'

'Couldn't you go later?' pleaded Lizzie. 'The next bus isn't for another hour.'

'OK, then.' Jane chewed her lip. 'It's just that I need to be at the stables in, like, half an hour. Charlie's coming out with us. We're going to ride over to Harlesgrove Woods.'

Lizzie grinned. 'No contest,' she teased. 'My needs against your love life!'

'Lizzie, for heaven's sake,' Jane snapped, to Lizzie's amazement. 'Leave it, OK?'

'Sorry.'

'No, I'm sorry,' Jane said sighing. 'To be honest, I'm pretty nervous.'

'Why? Come on, admit it – you're worried he might not be falling as madly in love with you as you are with him,' Lizzie suggested.

'I'm not in love,' Jane muttered unconvincingly.

'And I'm not addicted to cream eggs,' Lizzie said, laughing. 'Go for it, I say. Charlie's a whole heap better than your usual choice.'

Jane said nothing, but just sighed and nibbled a fingernail.

'So what's the problem?'

'I'm not sure that my riding is up to cantering about in open country any more – last time, we just rode in the sand school and that felt kind of safe.'

'You'll be fine,' Lizzie assured her. 'Remember how you used to jump those hurdles and do all that bareback stuff?'

'That was when I was twelve, Lizzie,' Jane protested.

'You'll be fine,' Lizzie assured her again. 'Go for it – just think, you and Charlie galloping side by side across the countryside, hair streaming in the wind – just like in that *Pride and Prejudice* DVD. Sooo romantic!'

CHAPTER 5

'I find myself very unwell . . .'
(Jane Austen, *Pride and Prejudice*)

'IF ELIZABETH BENNET IS IN THE BUILDING, *WILL SHE PLEASE go at once to Student Services?'*

The tannoy boomed out across the atrium, as Lizzie was battling with the drinks machine during a mid-morning break in rehearsing Year 7. Two of the music staff were off with a tummy bug and Lizzie knew that if she gave it her all, she'd be able to persuade them to give her a good reference for the one thing she really wanted to do with her life.

'Elizabeth Bennet . . .'

'What can that be about?' she mused, thumping the machine in anattempt to dislodge a carton of apple juice.

'That's Elizabeth Bennet, needed as a matter of urgency in Student Services.' Something in the tone of voice caused Lizzie's heart to lurch into her throat. She grabbed the drink, hooked her bag over her shoulder and headed for the stairs.

'Shall I come with you?' Emily offered, trotting along behind her. 'Sounds serious.'

'Get real,' Lizzie said, trying to suppress her anxiety. 'I've probably dropped some music or something. I'll catch up with you in a bit, yeah, and we'll go into town?'

The reception area in Student Services was crowded with the usual lunch-hour mix of kids feigning sickness in order to get an afternoon off to enjoy the heatwave, and others claiming a variety of lost and confiscated possessions. As Lizzie approached the desk, Mrs Carr, one of the receptionists, looked up, leaped to her feet and came towards her.

'Elizabeth, dear, I don't want you to worry,' she began, which filled Lizzie with even more alarm. 'But there's been a bit of an accident.'

'Not Mum and Dad!' Lizzie gasped, thinking of the way they had dashed off at high speed that morning.

'No, no . . .'

'The twins? Oh God, has Lydia done something stupid – the rock climbing?'

'Elizabeth, calm down,' Mrs Carr replied. 'No, it's your sister Jane. Apparently someone tried to call your mobile and when they couldn't reach you they phoned me. I did explain that you're not allowed to have phones on in school.'

'So – what happened? Where is she?'

'I'm not sure of the details, something about falling off a horse and —'

'Oh no – is she OK?'

'She's been taken to the General Hospital,' Mrs Carr said, handing Lizzie a slip of paper. 'This is the phone number of the man who left the message.'

Lizzie glanced at the paper. The number didn't mean anything to her, but she guessed it must be Charlie's.

'He said he'd called round at your house, but there was no one there.'

'My parents are away,' Lizzie said. 'I've got to go. I need to see her.'

'Of course you do,' Mrs Carr said.

'And can you let my sister know? Meredith – 11C?'

'Of course. And I'm sure Jane will be fine. By the time you get there, she'll probably be on her way home!'

As the taxi edged across a stream of traffic and turned into the hospital forecourt, Lizzie punched the number she had been given into her phone one last time.

'I'm sorry, but the person you are calling is not available . . .'

She snapped the phone shut and sighed. She guessed that Charlie was at the hospital with Jane where his phone would have to be switched off. She felt so guilty – she'd been the one to persuade Jane that riding would be fine. If anything really bad had happened, she'd never forgive herself.

She thrust a five-pound note into the taxi driver's hand, slammed the door, and ran up the ramp and through the automatic doors into the Accident and Emergency department.

'I'm looking for Jane Bennet, she's my sister,' she panted to the first nurse. 'Can I see her? Is she badly hurt?'

'Just take a seat and I'll get the doctor.' The nurse gestured towards a row of chairs against the wall.

'Please can you just tell me how she is?'

'She could be a lot worse.' At the sound of a deep gravelly voice behind her, Lizzie spun round.

And found herself face-to-face with James Darcy.

'What are you doing here?' she gasped, as the nurse headed down the corridor. 'Where's Charlie? He phoned.'

'He didn't; I did. I thought you'd want to know. I tried your phone, but it was off so I rang the school.'

For a moment, Lizzie was lost for words. But only for a moment.

'But how did you know my number?'

The faintest glimmer of a smile crossed James's face.

'Jane's phone – it was obvious she'd have her own sister's mobile programmed in. It wasn't rocket science. And since she was out cold . . .'

'Oh my God!' Lizzie's face blanched as she clamped a hand to her mouth.

'Only for a second, it wasn't that dramatic,' James said.

'That's OK for you to say, she's not your sister!'

'Sit.' James pushed her down on to one of the chairs. 'Can you keep quiet long enough for me to tell you what happened? Or is that too much to expect?'

On any other occasion his sarcasm would have enraged her, but she was in no position to argue.

'Caroline took Jane out riding this morning.'

'So – wasn't Charlie there?'

'Clearly keeping quiet is a skill you haven't mastered as yet.'

'Maybe if you could just get to the point,' she retorted.

'He was meant to go,' James said, 'but at the last

moment his mother wanted him to go with her to see – well, there was family business to attend to.'

He chewed his lip for a second and then went on.

'The whole thing was an accident waiting to happen, if you ask me,' he said, shaking his head. 'It's obvious Jane's a total novice around horses and Caro put her on Lottie, who apparently gets spooked by the slightest thing.' He stifled a yawn. 'Stupid girl.'

'My sister is not stupid, she just hasn't had much experience.'

'I was referring to Caroline, actually. Anyway, from what I can gather, a combine harvester started up in the field nearby, Lottie bolted, Jane came off, hit her head on a fence post and by the look of it knackered her wrist as well.'

He glanced at Lizzie's ashen face. 'She'll no doubt survive,' he muttered. 'So please don't go all hysterical on me.'

'Do you know something? You are totally unbelievable!' Lizzie replied angrily. 'If I wasn't so worried about – oh! Doctor.'

She leaped to her feet as a guy in a white coat with a stethoscope slung round his neck came towards her.

'Are you Jane Bennet's family?' he asked.

'I am, he's not,' Lizzie said, moving away from James. 'She is going to be OK, isn't she?'

'She'll be fine,' he said. 'But we're keeping her here for a few more hours, because she was unconscious for a minute or two. She's been sick, but that could just be the shock. And she does seem a bit confused – that's the bit we need to watch.'

Lizzie stared at him. She'd watched enough episodes of *House* and *Holby City* to know what he was hinting at.

'Can I see her?' The words came out as a high-pitched squeak.

'Sure,' he said. 'Cubicle nine. And don't worry about the lump on her head – that's a good sign.'

'Lizzie?'

Jane's eyes flickered open as Lizzie pulled a chair up to her bed.

'Yes, it's me,' Lizzie said, shocked at the total lack of colour in her sister's face apart from the livid violet lump above her left eye.

'Head hurts,' Jane mumbled. 'What's going on?'

'You fell off the horse, remember?' Lizzie replied, taking her hand.

Jane groaned and shut her eyes.

'But it's OK, you're going to be just fine.'

'Can I get you anything?' James hovered in the doorway, his expression a whole heap gentler than usual. 'Coffee?'

'Who'sat?' Jane's speech was slurred as she struggled to focus without her contacts. 'Simon? Simon – darling? You came.'

'It's not Simon, silly . . .' Lizzie began.

'Si – love you . . . oh.'

Jane's eyes rolled in her head and she began to gag. Lizzie grabbed one of the cardboard bowls near the trolley just in time.

'James, quick, get a nurse,' she cried.

But James had already disappeared.

* * *

When the porters arrived an hour later to take Jane off to X-ray, Lizzie dashed outside to try to phone her parents. There was no reply from either her mum's phone or her father's BlackBerry; the hotel said they hadn't checked in yet, but that didn't surprise her since her father would doubtless be insisting on visiting every antiquarian bookshop in London while he had the chance.

There was a text from Meredith begging to know what was happening, but when Lizzie tried her phone it was switched off and she had to leave a message at reception. There were times when school rules were, she considered, a total pain in the butt.

She was trying her mum's phone again when she spotted a familiar figure loping across the car park towards her.

'I just heard,' Charlie panted, taking the steps two at a time. A damp strand of hair was flopping over one eye, his T-shirt was half in and half out of his shorts and the expression on his face was like a small boy whose dog had been caught chasing sheep. 'How is she? I'll kill my sister – what was she thinking of? I'm so sorry.'

'It wasn't your fault,' Lizzie assured him.

'So – your parents are here, yes?' Charlie asked as they walked back into the hospital. 'They must be incandescent with us.'

Lizzie shook her head and explained about their trip.

'And I can't reach them,' she sighed, walking up to the Triage desk. 'James is here, though.'

'Really? He's still here? That's pretty decent of him,

considering.' Charlie nodded thoughtfully.

'Considering what?' Lizzie demanded, looking around for someone who might give her news of Jane. 'That it meant spending time in the company of people he loathes?'

'What?' Charlie replied, frowning at her. 'It's just that he hates hospitals, that's all.'

'Oh, and of course, the rest of us absolutely love them,' Lizzie said, and then checked herself, catching the bemused expression on Charlie's face.

'But it was nice of him to hang around, I guess,' she added grudgingly.

As if summoned by the mention of his name, the swing doors opened and James appeared, clutching two polystyrene cups of coffee. 'So you got here?' he remarked, nodding at Charlie. 'Everything OK with your – well, you know?'

'Sure. Fine.' Charlie's tone was clipped and dismissive. 'So – have you seen Jane?'

'Yes.' James glanced at his watch, which Lizzie couldn't help noticing was a Patek Philippe and very swish.

'And?' Charlie urged.

James shrugged. 'I reckon she's OK,' he replied. 'They were wheeling her back from X-ray when I went to get coffee and she recognised me and managed to string sentences together. So assuming she's avoided MRSA, which in a dump like this would be an achievement in itself, I guess the crisis is over.'

He thrust one of the cups into Lizzie's hands and turned to Charlie.

'So – can we go?'

'Go?' Charlie repeated incredulously. 'No way – not

till I've seen Jane.'

'It's not your problem,' James replied. 'She'll want her family, not – well, not a load of strangers.'

'I'm not a stranger,' Charlie retorted, colouring slightly. 'Well, not really.'

'I'm sure Janey'd love to see you,' Lizzie assured him, if only to contradict James. 'I'll go and check things out.'

'Lizzie!'

She turned to find Meredith running towards her, her school bag bouncing on her bony hip.

'How is she? What's happened?' Before Lizzie could reply, Meredith had wheeled round to face Charlie. 'How could you let this happen? If she dies —'

'Meredith, for heaven's sake!' Lizzie burst out. 'She's not going to die and it wasn't Charlie's fault. It was an accident.'

'So did she have a hard hat? If she didn't sign a disclaimer, she can sue you, you know – Health and Safety and —'

'Give me strength,' James muttered under his breath.

'Meredith, shut it!' Lizzie hissed.

'Elizabeth Bennet?' A lanky registrar in a slightly grubby white coat beckoned from one of the cubicles. 'Your sister's back from X-ray and asking for you.'

Silently Lizzie gave thanks for the perfect timing.

'The X-ray showed nothing sinister, and she's much brighter now,' the registrar went on. 'We'll keep her here for a few hours to be on the safe side, but then she should be OK to go home. And that wrist – badly sprained, and a torn ligament to boot, but no fracture. So all in all, good news.'

'Thank you,' Lizzie breathed with a sigh of relief.

She grabbed Meredith's arm.

'Come on, let's go and see her. You coming?' she added, turning to Charlie.

'Only two in a cubicle at a time, I'm afraid,' the doctor cautioned her.

'Give her my love, then, yeah?' Charlie asked anxiously.

'Sure, 'course I will,' Lizzie grinned. She turned to follow the doctor, who was already striding towards the curtained cubicles. Which was why she didn't hear James's muttered remark.

'Frankly, Charlie, I wouldn't waste your time.'

CHAPTER 6

'She attracted him more than he liked . . .'
(Jane Austen, *Pride and Prejudice*)

'I FEEL SUCH A FOOL. I'VE REALLY MESSED THINGS UP.'

Jane winced slightly as she slid off the bed and began walking with Lizzie and Meredith towards the hospital exit at seven o'clock that evening. Her wrist was bandaged and in a sling, and the bruise on her forehead was turning an even more interesting shade of violet, but the doctor had assured Lizzie that Jane was fit to be discharged.

'Why do you feel a fool? It wasn't your fault,' Meredith remarked, averting her eyes from a vomiting four-year-old in the corridor.

'Exactly – even James admitted that,' Lizzie reasoned. 'And just think – it might even have been worth it. You get to spend a night under the same roof as Charlie.'

She had been pretty miffed when Charlie and James had disappeared before she could get Charlie in to see Jane, but when the nurse had handed her a phone message from Vanessa, promising to fetch them and look after Jane till her parents got home, Lizzie guessed that it was all Charlie's doing.

'I can't go,' groaned Jane, pausing and giving her sister a pleading look. 'I mean, it's ever so kind of Charlie's mum to suggest it, but I hardly know them and it's so grand.'

'No buts,' Lizzie ordered. 'Mrs Bingley's already on her way – she's dropping us off at home and then taking you to Netherfield. Think about it, it's destiny. Charlie will see you looking all wan and pathetic, and all his testosterone will go on red alert!'

'That is so not going to happen,' her sister protested. 'They'll all just see me as a wimp who couldn't sit on a horse. Why don't I just come home with you?'

'Because,' Lizzie said, 'it's all arranged – and anyway, Mum would be devastated.'

Mrs Bennet, who had initially been panic-stricken at the news of Jane's fall and threatened to come home that very instant, had calmed down considerably when Lizzie announced that Mrs Bingley was insisting that Jane spent the night at Netherfield.

'For one thing,' Vanessa had told Lizzie firmly, 'it's because of us that poor Jane had the accident in the first place, and secondly, what if she had a relapse in the night? You can't be too careful and you don't want the responsibility on your shoulders. I insist.'

When Lizzie had related all this to her mother, Mrs Bennet had almost purred with satisfaction. 'This could be the making of our relationship with the Bingleys,' she had said. 'And so useful, coming at this time.'

'What are you on about, Mum?' Lizzie had sighed.

'Drew's visit, of course,' her mother replied. 'If we play our cards right, Charlie and – oh, the other young man, whatever his name is – talks with a plum in his mouth . . .'

'James.'

'Yes, well, those two can take him out and about. Keep him out of our hair.'

'Mum, it's nothing to do with them.'

'Be good for Drew to see the circles we move in – that Felicity was always bragging about the people she knew – and besides, we could make things very unpleasant for the Bingleys – not that we would, but they don't know that.'

At which point Lizzie had brought the conversation to an abrupt halt under the pretext of having to speak to the doctor.

'Well,' Jane sighed as they collected her discharge letter from the nurses' station and headed for the exit, 'couldn't you stay at Netherfield too?'

'No, p . . . please,' Meredith stammered, her face creased in a frown that sent her glasses shooting down her nose.

'It's OK,' Lizzie assured her. 'Meredith hasn't been invited, and I don't blame her for not wanting to be in the house on her own.'

She knew that despite coming across as a pompous pain a lot of the time, Meredith was scared of three things: global warming, food additives and the dark.

'Sorry, I forgot about the twins being away,' Jane sighed, as a silver Mercedes with an anxious-looking Vanessa Bingley at the wheel pulled into the hospital forecourt and stopped in front of a No Parking sign. 'OK – but first thing tomorrow, I'm coming home, no matter what.'

* * *

'So when did you last eat?' Vanessa demanded of Lizzie as she accelerated out of the hospital entrance.

'Um – can't remember,' Lizzie admitted, suddenly conscious of the hollowness of her stomach now that Jane was OK.

'I guessed as much,' Vanessa nodded. 'Well, you'll eat with us. I say us – not me, of course, because I'm off out to my dramatic society rehearsal – *Abigail's Party*, such fun!'

'Honestly, it's very kind, but there's no need,' Lizzie began, as Meredith caught her eye and pulled a face. 'It's too hot to eat much anyway.'

'I'm not listening,' declared Vanessa. 'My lot are barbecuing and what's an extra sausage one way or the other?'

She raised a hand as Lizzie opened her mouth to protest further.

'And now then, I meant to ask. Are any of you any good with paint?'

'Well, what else could I say?' Jane demanded, while Mrs Bingley had parked and popped into the village shop for a bottle of wine. 'Mum *is* arty and she'd be in her element.'

'Designing backdrops?' Lizzie queried and then sighed. 'More importantly, being let loose with this am-dram lot? Can't you just see her? She can't do two hours at a party without being a total embarrassment!'

'Lizzie, lighten up,' Jane said, wincing slightly and running her hand across her forehead.

'Oh God, are you OK?' Lizzie gasped. 'Have you got a

headache? Do you feel sick? The doctor said —'

'No, but I've just remembered,' Jane said. 'The school concert – it's tonight and you should be there. I've wrecked it for you.'

'You're more important,' Lizzie assured her. 'I've done all the important stuff. I was only going to be there to help the kids get made up – and there are plenty of other people around to do that.'

She eyed Jane anxiously, desperate not to let her disappointment at missing the concert show on her face.

'Are you sure you're feeling all right?'

'I'm fine,' Jane replied. 'Just tired. And wishing I didn't have to face Caroline and Charlie tonight. Trouble is, I bet they feel just the same about me.'

As Lizzie dashed up the stairs at their house to collect Jane's pyjamas and wash bag, her mobile, stuffed into the back pocket of her jeans, began to vibrate.

'Hello?'

It was Emily.

'I've done it, oh my God, I've done it,' she gabbled. 'And I so have to know what he's thinking, but I daren't call, because I've got to help out at the concert, so, like, if you phone him and kind of ask . . .'

'Emily, what the hell are you talking about?' Lizzie demanded, wedging the phone between her ear and her left shoulder and rummaging in Jane's chest of drawers.

'Toby, silly!' Emily replied. 'I've emailed an invite to my party, right? I tried to make it sound kind of mysterious, only now I'm not sure —'

'I can't talk now, Emily,' Lizzie interrupted. 'Bit of a crisis

– that's why I wasn't at the concert. You see, Jane's —'

'Oh, right. So not only do you disappear and not let me know where you are, but now you're saying you don't want to help me. You don't want him, but no one else can have him, is that it? Well, stuff you!'

'*Emily!*' Lizzie shouted. 'Will you just —?'

But Emily had hung up.

The idea of a barbecue had bitten the dust within minutes of the girls arriving at Netherfield. The heavy stillness of the late afternoon had given way to a stiff breeze, then to a few raindrops and by the time they had reached the front door, the distant rumble of thunder announced the arrival of the storm that the Met Office had been predicting for days. Within minutes, rain was cascading off the conservatory roof and dripping from the huge umbrella on the terrace. As a result, supper had been cooked in the Aga and they had all eaten round the kitchen table. Charlie sat next to Jane and at least twice, Lizzie spotted his hand reaching for her sister's and noticed the way Jane coloured as their eyes met.

Whether it was the effect of the large glass of white wine Charlie had pressed on her, or the embarrassment of Meredith's constant enquiries as to why the Bingleys didn't have more low energy light bulbs in their vast kitchen, by nine o'clock Lizzie was feeling rather guilty. For one thing, Caroline, far from being the snooty little madam of the previous weekend, seemed genuinely upset and concerned about Jane, to the point of recounting several occasions when she herself had fallen off horses and saying it was all the fault of the driver of the combine and nothing to do with Jane's ability as a horsewoman. Charlie had taken the trouble to fish out a whole pile of *Countryside Today* magazines for Meredith, and Mrs Bingley, prior to dashing off to her rehearsal, had insisted on phoning Lizzie's parents to reassure them that Jane was in safe hands. They were, she decided, a lot nicer as a family than she had first thought.

Which was more than could be said for James. About James, she knew she'd been right from the start. At supper, he had hardly said more than two words, and paid more attention to the family's three dogs – a bouncy red setter and two flat coat retrievers – than to any of the human visitors; and on three separate occasions, Lizzie had caught him staring at her through narrowed eyes, his upper lip curled in a sardonic half-smile that suggested he found her hugely amusing in a patronising sort of way. She had a huge urge to thump him between the eyes.

The moment the meal was over, he had got up and without a word left the room, shutting the door into what Lizzie assumed was the sitting room firmly behind him. Caroline, spotting Jane desperately trying to suppress a yawn, had insisted, not only on taking her upstairs to the guest room, but waiting outside the bathroom in case she felt faint while taking a shower. Charlie had taken Meredith down the garden to see the new wildflower wilderness and bug boxes that their conservation-mad gardener had recently installed.

Which left Lizzie momentarily on her own.

Why she immediately got up from the table and walked through to the sitting room, she had no idea. Later, she tried to convince herself that it was because she had heard the music, but that wasn't true; it wasn't until she pushed open the door that she heard the strains of a crystal-clear soprano voice singing. For a moment, it seemed that the vast room, furnished with deep sofas, antique occasional tables and, in the far corner, a baby grand piano, was empty; but then, turning towards the double doors that led on to the terrace, she saw him. James was standing with his back to her, his forehead pressed against the glass, motionless.

For an instant, she just stood and looked at him. His hair curled into the nape of his neck, his shorts were tight across his bum and the backs of his legs had a hint of sunburn. For some reason, this pleased her hugely – an even suntan would have been just too perfect.

The track on the CD came to an end, and James turned, caught sight of her, and stood for a second as if in freeze-frame.

'That's a beautiful song,' Lizzie said, embarrassed by her own intrusion. 'I've not heard that setting before – but I did sing the Rutter version at a concert last month.'

James's eyes widened. 'You sing? What, classical stuff like this? Really?'

Again, that note of disbelief and incredulity, which rankled even more than his unspoken suggestion that classical music was so much more worthwhile than any other kind.

'Yes, I do,' she replied. 'And I play the French horn and the piano – funnily enough, even state-school kids can enjoy music – isn't that amazing?'

'OK, can we sort this?' James said. 'I'm sorry if what I said about your school annoyed you, but believe me, I had my reasons. It's just that – well, I had some pretty grim experiences at the hands of state-school kids.'

'And because of that, you label all of us?'

'I've apologised, haven't I?' he snapped. 'Charlie thinks I'm a snob, but I'm not. Things have happened to make me feel like I do – and once I've made up my mind about something, that's it.'

'That is so arrogant,' Lizzie cried. 'That's like saying you're never wrong.'

'I'm not very often,' he said and then smiled ruefully. 'So tell me – you sing in a choir?'

'Two,' Lizzie replied curtly. 'School and church.'

'And you liked the CD?'

Lizzie nodded. 'Beautiful,' she said, grateful to change the subject before she said something she knew she'd end up regretting. 'Can I see the case? I'd like to buy it.'

'Well, actually, you can't, because —' James stopped in mid-sentence as the door burst open and Caroline came in.

'*There* you are!' she exclaimed, all semblance of friendliness evaporating as she glanced from James to Lizzie. 'Jane's going to bed. She wants to see you.'

'Thanks, I'll go up and then we must leave,' Lizzie replied pleasantly. She turned to James.

'The title of the CD?' she urged.

'I'll text you the details,' James said evasively. 'Good night.'

Lizzie turned and walked from the room. As she pulled the door closed behind her, she caught Caroline's words.

'That girl is unbelievable! What a cheek, marching in here and bothering you.'

What Lizzie didn't hear, as she stomped upstairs, her blood boiling, was James's reply.

'Who said I was bothered?'

'For someone who couldn't wait to get home, you took your time,' Lizzie teased Jane the following morning. 'Mum's just texted to say they're at Milton Keynes – they'll be here in half an hour.'

'Mmm.'

'Jane, you've got a soppy grin on your face. Go on, tell me all!'

'There's nothing to tell,' Jane replied.

'Jane!'

'OK, so he's lovely. I really, really like him, Lizzie.' She sighed. 'I mean, he's not like other guys. I kind of don't have to try with him. I can just be me. But . . .' She paused.

'But what? Sounds like a dream come true to me,' Lizzie said laughing.

'I felt like that about Simon, and look what happened there,' Jane said. 'Charlie's probably just being polite and I'm reading too much into it.'

'Come off it, what guy in the twenty-first century does *anything* they don't want to do? If he's being cool with you, it's because he fancies you something chronic.'

'You think so?' Jane asked eagerly.

'Trust me. If there's one thing I'm good at, it's reading people. Charlie Bingley is putty in your hands.'

❧ CHAPTER 7 ❧

'Collins was not a sensible man.'
(Jane Austen, *Pride and Prejudice*)

'THAT DREW IS UNREAL!' LYDIA DECLARED, FLOPPING down on one of the wicker chairs on the patio late on Saturday afternoon, and unscrewing the top of her new black nail polish.

'Absolutely,' Katie agreed.

'Does he ever shut up, I wonder?' Lizzie sighed, rubbing sunscreen into her legs.

'Oh, come on,' Jane broke in on her sisters' moans, 'he's probably just nervous. I mean, imagine us arriving in a strange country and having to stay with people we didn't know.'

'It's not that strange,' Lizzie pointed out, as the strains of *Lohengrin* wafted through the open window from their father's newly designated music room. 'After all, he lived here till he was ten, for heaven's sake.'

'And he didn't exactly seem fazed by anything, did he?' Lydia added, plonking her foot on Katie's lap and starting to paint her toenails. 'Oh but I forgot, he's "*right-hand man to one of America's most venerated hoteliers*".'

She imitated Drew's Boston drawl, which reduced her sisters to giggles.

'Be quiet,' Jane pleaded, wincing slightly with the pain from her wrist. 'He'll hear us.'

'No, he won't,' Lizzie laughed. 'He's upstairs, "abluting".'

'I hadn't a clue what he was on about,' Katie said. 'Why couldn't he just ask to take a shower?'

Ever since their parents had arrived home at ten that morning, with Drew Collins and enough luggage to keep him in clean clothes for a year, the girls had had the utmost difficulty in keeping straight faces. Drew was twenty-two, but acted thirty-five; tall, stockily built and with one of the most unfortunate haircuts Lizzie had ever seen, he had eyes that appeared too small for his face and a mouth that was not only too large, but never stopped working.

He also had a very inflated opinion of himself.

'Oh, don't you worry about a single little thing,' he had declared when Mrs Bennet showed him into the spacious guest room with its en-suite shower and said, through gritted teeth, that she hoped he'd be comfortable. 'I'm able to bunk down just anywhere I find myself. Just because I'm used to some of the top hotels in the world, don't mean I can't enjoy a little basic living now and then. I'm a very adaptable kinda guy.'

And over supper, the family had been subjected to his views on nutrition.

'Now I just want you to know that I'm not your typical stereotype American guy,' he had declared. 'No junk food comes near my body; so I won't be trying your fish and chips, nor your Yorkshire pudding. But I don't want you to worry; just because I'm used to eating food in some of the top hotels . . .'

He had then listed the various food items he could not consume (this took some time because each item was accompanied by a graphic description of the effect it had on various parts of his anatomy). Then he sighed with relief when Mrs Bennet assured him that yes, whenever possible she bought organic food and that while the tap water in their area was perfectly drinkable, if he really insisted, she would purchase a large quantity of sparkling spring water the very next day. That being settled, he then polished off two helpings of shepherd's pie, a large bowl of strawberries and whipped cream, two wedges of Stilton cheese and the larger part of a bunch of grapes.

'Tell us,' Mr Bennet had said, when Drew had paused briefly to take a breath, 'about your hotel management course.'

'I am so excited,' Drew had replied, laying down his spoon and beaming at them all. 'I was named Trainee of the Year (Eastern Seaboard) because – guess what? My exceptional talent for management was spotted by no less than KDB herself!'

He had leaned back so far in his chair that he almost fell into the yucca plant standing at the side of the hearth.

'The KGB?' Katie had gasped, her eyes like saucers. 'Isn't that the people who chase criminals?'

'No, no, no!' Drew had laughed. 'Kay Dee Bee – Katrina De Burgh. Of De Burgh Hotels. My employers. She's the granddaughter of the founder and the new CEO.'

'Fascinating,' Mr Bennet had murmured solemnly. 'And your talent is so great that this lady felt Europe should benefit from it?'

Drew coloured slightly as the girls struggled to suppress their giggles.

'Well, of course, I'm not one to brag, but Mrs De Burgh being half English – well, Scottish, I believe – really warmed to me; and then again, I am a very fast learner, which is why she's earmarked me for fast-track management training. And part of that is a placement in Europe.'

'Where exactly?' Jane had asked politely, kicking Lizzie under the table as she stifled a yawn.

'*Château de la Belle Rose*,' he pronounced with a flourish, but without a trace of anything approaching a French accent. 'In France. The latest acquisition for the De Burgh Luxury Living portfolio. So in three weeks I shall have to leave you and be on my way.'

'Three?' gasped Lizzie's mum. 'Harry, you said two and —'

'Oh, but I forgot,' Drew exclaimed, cutting her short. 'I have a little treat for you, in gratitude for your hospitality.' He paused, presumably to allow the excitement to build. 'Vouchers for a two-night-stay, including a half-day's pampering in the spa at any De Burgh hotel in the UK,' he declared, handing Alice a gold envelope.

Lizzie winked at Jane as their mother clearly wavered between her excitement at the thought of five-star living and her unwillingness to express indebtedness to Drew.

'Well, that's very kind,' she murmured. 'Oh, look, a

list of hotels – Brighton, Bath, Edinburgh – oh, Harry, I fancy Edinburgh!'

'But Brighton is so close to Glyndebourne,' Harry replied. 'We could do the opera.'

A glare from his wife put an end to further discussion. 'There's a spa and a pool and – ooh, look, four-poster beds!'

'Edinburgh it is, then,' sighed Harry. 'Most kind. Now Drew, I'm sure the jet lag must be catching up with you, so perhaps you'd like to go to your room and rest?'

'Oh, I sure don't get jet lag,' said Drew. 'When you've been on as many business class flights as I have . . .'

At which point, Mr Bennet urgently remembered a phone call he simply had to make, Katie and Lydia discovered a sudden urge to begin their school holiday projects, and Mrs Bennet decided this was the moment to return Mrs Bingley's phone call about theatre backdrops. Lizzie had offered to clear the table and Jane, on the pretext of an aching wrist, had hurried upstairs in search of painkillers, leaving Meredith to bombard Drew with questions about what De Burgh hotels were doing to be eco-friendly, and holding forth about sourcing food that was locally grown and organic. Listening to their intense conversation through the dining-room hatch, it had occurred to Lizzie that if there was a prize for being boring, it would be a close-run contest between Drew and her sister.

'Done!' declared Lydia now, examining her toenails with satisfaction. 'I'm off to get changed. You coming, Katie?'

Her sister's eyes widened.

'With you? To Amber's?' she asked eagerly. 'For the evening?'

'Sure – why not? A whole crowd's going to meet for a barbie in the Forsters' garden – her mum's out with the new man at some ball or other. Who knows – I might find you a guy.' She made it sound about as likely as snow in August.

'But has Amber said it's OK?' Katie ventured. Amber was known throughout Meryton Academy for her scathing remarks to anyone she deemed unfit to be in her clique and Katie had on many occasions been the butt of her sarcasm.

Lydia laughed. 'She'll do whatever I say,' she replied. 'She owes me. Now are you coming or not?'

'You bet! But – what shall I wear?'

'White cropped jeans, that bright orange shirt and those shiny bronze slingbacks I told you to buy. And don't be long or I'll go without you.'

As Katie, grinning from ear to ear, dashed into the house, swiftly followed by Lydia shouting instructions about earrings and make-up, Jane turned to Lizzie.

'You know, I think Lyddy is actually getting to be nicer to Katie,' she remarked. 'I mean, she didn't have to invite her tonight. It's not like she's in Amber's set.'

'Too right,' Lizzie nodded. 'And if you ask me there's only one reason why she has.'

'Which is?'

'She wants something. Lydia always has an ulterior motive.'

Before Jane could reply, Lydia was back.

'Look who's here!' she cried. 'Lover boy!'

Jane's face flushed scarlet as Charlie Bingley hovered in the doorway of the conservatory.

Lydia giggled and puckered her lips in a kiss behind Charlie's back.

'And look, he's got chocolates! Sweet or what?'

It was as Lizzie got up, suppressing the desire to throttle her sister on the spot, that she saw Charlie wasn't alone.

Standing behind him, eyeing Lydia with complete disdain and swinging a tennis racket, was James Darcy. Dressed in crisp white shorts and an open neck polo shirt that revealed just a smattering of chest hair, even Lizzie had to admit he was – in an arrogant, distant kind of way – very fit.

'You do like chocolates?' Charlie asked anxiously, handing the box to Jane. 'I know it's a pretty naff idea, and it's so damn hot they've probably melted but . . .'

'They're my favourite,' Jane assured him, taking the box from him as Lydia, blowing another fake kiss, scuttled off. 'That's really kind.'

There was an awkward pause as Jane looked first at her feet, then out of the window and finally, biting her lip, turned back to Charlie. 'Um – would you like a drink? There's some of Meredith's home-made lemonade in the kitchen. Unlike some of her culinary efforts, it's pretty good.'

'No thanks, we're just off to play tennis,' James said, turning as if to leave.

'There's no rush,' Charlie replied. 'The court's not booked for another half-hour.'

'I'll fetch it,' Jane said. 'Oh —' She waggled her

bandaged wrist in the air. 'Lizzie, can you . . .?'

'No problem, I'll help,' Charlie said at once. 'Lead on!'

'This is for you.' James tossed a brown padded envelope at Lizzie as Jane and Charlie disappeared into the house. 'The CD – I burned one for you.'

Lizzie looked at him in astonishment. 'You did? Thank you,' she said, ripping open the envelope and taking the disc out. 'Hey, – it's blank. I mean, you haven't written the name of the artist or anything.'

'Oh. Well, no. I mean, she's hardly an artist.'

'I thought she was brilliant,' Lizzie said.

'Really?' James queried, his face breaking into the nearest thing to a genuine grin that Lizzie had yet seen. 'I'll tell her. She'll be thrilled.'

'You know this woman? So who is she?' asked Lizzie. 'What's her name? I'd like to hear some of her other stuff.'

'She's called Jenna Darcy. She's my sister. And there isn't any more.'

'She's . . . you never said you had a sister.'

'You never asked.'

'So tell me about her? Is she at school? College? Does she sing with a choir?'

James paused, tossed his racket onto the patio table and took a deep breath. 'The thing about Jenna,' he began, 'is that she's been —'

He started, as the conservatory door burst open.

'Well, hi there! Jane said we had visitors!'

Lizzie cringed as Drew, wearing ankle-basher trousers and with his hair so heavily gelled that he looked like a frightened hedgehog, strode across the patio towards them.

'How ya doing?' To Lizzie's horror, he actually slapped James on the back. 'I'm Drew Collins, visiting from the US of A. And you are?'

'This is James Darcy,' Lizzie said with a sigh.

'Well, James, I guess Lizzie's told you all about me.'

'No.' James eyed him up and down with visible distaste.

'Ah. Well, I'm a close family friend from Massachusetts,' Drew declared. 'My pa and Lizzie's parents were in business together way back. It all went badly wrong, thanks to Harry not being quite on the ball, but hey, no hard feelings.'

'That is so not the way it was,' Lizzie burst out. 'My father worked his guts out to save the business while Ambrose —'

'God rest his soul.' Drew closed his eyes momentarily and Lizzie felt a cow. The guy was, after all, dead and presumably all Drew was doing was trying to rewrite history to make things look better.

'Sorry. It's all in the past anyway.'

'And you two are an item, I guess?' Drew's mournful expression disappeared as rapidly as it had come.

'No way!' Lizzie burst out, horrified at the audacity of the guy. 'We hardly know one another.'

'Really?'

'Really,' James repeated. 'Absolutely not.'

'Aw man! Wow! Well. Gee.'

To which neither Lizzie nor James had any answer at all. Fortunately the ensuing, rather awkward, silence was broken by the arrival of Emily, who came bursting through the back gate in her usual state of sweaty disarray.

'Sorry, sorry, a million zillion sorries – oh, sorry!' She caught sight of James and Drew and pulled a face. 'Am I interrupting?'

'It's fine,' Lizzie assured her. 'And what's with all the apologies?'

'For being so crabby,' Emily replied. 'You know, over the Toby thing. I bumped into Lydia and she told me about Jane's accident. No wonder you weren't in the mood to talk.'

'It was pretty full on,' Lizzie agreed, 'but I should have rung back.'

'Well, you couldn't have done anything about it anyway because he's not coming. He'll be away. Just my luck.'

She sighed and pulled Lizzie to one side. 'Can't stop – going babysitting, but I'm so fed up. Everything about my party's going wrong,' she muttered. 'I want it to be great, but it's so not going to happen. Mum's insisting on totally the wrong food, Dad wants it all upmarket and formal, and as for me – what a loser I'm going to look with no boyfriend and spots the size of pistachio nuts.'

She paused, eyeing Drew. 'Who's that?'

'This is Drew Collins,' Lizzie explained hurriedly, relieved to have a reason to deflect Emily from her rapid descent into self-pity. 'From America. He's staying with us for a bit.'

'Hi,' Emily grinned. 'Will you be around Saturday week? Cos if so, you're invited too. James and Charlie'll be there and Denny and, oh, of course, you won't know these guys. Well, anyway . . .'

Lizzie wished that Emily wouldn't go into overdrive every time she met a new guy.

'I'd sure like that,' Drew replied. 'What sort of party is it?'

'My eighteenth,' Emily said.

'No, no, I mean what's the theme?' Drew went on. 'All the best parties have a theme – or at least, that's the way we do them where I come from.'

'Which is Milton Keynes originally, isn't it?' Lizzie asked sweetly as Jane and Charlie finally appeared from the kitchen.

'A theme! Oh my God – I never thought about anything like that,' Emily groaned. 'Got to dash, but – talk later, Drew, yeah?'

She waved and belted out of the back gate, only narrowly missing crashing into Charlie, who was carrying a tray of drinks.

'Sorry we've been so long,' Charlie said. 'Oh, hi, Emily – oh, bye, Emily!'

He dumped the tray on the patio table and began handing round glasses.

'Listen, you lot – we've cooked up the greatest scheme.' He turned to James. 'Your aunt's horse is running next Saturday at Newmarket, right?

'No, Brighton, actually – it's a big charity race day affair,' James replied. 'Newmarket's next month.'

'Oh yeah, that's right, Brighton. Denny said,' Charlie acknowledged.

'Denny?' James frowned.

'Yes, the college is sponsoring a race, apparently – and they've got a stand there, you know, promoting their courses and stuff. Anyway, it was Denny that gave me the idea. How about we all go over for the day? I know Caro would be up for it. She's still miffed about missing Ascot because of that bug she caught.'

For once, James looked mildly enthusiastic.

'Could be cool,' he nodded. 'Since the sainted aunt's in France with Jenna, that leaves me.'

'With Jenna?' Lizzie cut in. 'So is your sister —'

'Wow, the races sure does sound a neat idea,' Drew burst out. 'Count me in.'

Lizzie flinched inwardly at his audacity.

'Oh, sorry – I don't think we've met,' Charlie replied, glancing at Jane.

'This is Drew,' Jane explained and went through the introductions once again.

'So come on, James,' Charlie urged. 'What do you say? Up for it?'

'I guess,' he said. 'I'll have to sort passes for the Owners' stand, though – how many of us are going?'

'Me, Jane . . .'

'No, I'll pass on that one,' Jane said quickly.

'No way!' Charlie exclaimed. 'That's the whole point – I mean, you said you thought it'd be fun.'

'Yes, but you said Newmarket.'

'So? What's the difference?' Charlie demanded.

Lizzie knew exactly what the difference was. Brighton was where Simon lived and went to college. Brighton was where Jane and he had hung out, weekend after weekend. Brighton, regardless of what Jane pretended, was still full of memories her sister would rather forget.

'Please.' Charlie looked pleadingly at Jane.

'If she doesn't want to go, she doesn't want to go,' James snapped. 'Just because you and I are into that kind of stuff . . .'

Jane took a deep breath. 'No, I'd like to go. Really. It'll be cool. Lizzie – you'll come too, yeah?'

'I don't know, I . . .'

'Oh, you must,' Charlie butted in. 'Caroline will be really miffed if you don't.'

Which served only to prove to Lizzie that, friendly as Charlie might be, he really didn't have a clue when it came to reading human nature.

After the guys had left, Lizzie went to her room and played the CD. It was obviously an amateur recording, but that couldn't disguise the fact that Jenna's voice had a haunting quality, as though the singer's heart was breaking with every note.

Suddenly the track stopped, and there was a lot of rustling. And then the first few bars of *Angry in Your Face*. Was this the same girl? Feisty, spunky, spitting out the lyrics and then abruptly dropping into a soft crooning of the refrain.

'*And one day, babe, I'll show you how, it feels to be, here, without you, now.*'

'Amazing!' Lizzie spoke the word out loud as she pressed the Rewind button. The range of her voice was astonishing and what was even more surprising was the fact that anyone related to James could sound so – well, abandoned, uninhibited – normal, in fact.

She found herself wondering just what it was that James had been going to reveal about Jenna when Drew had burst in on them.

And, despite her reservations about anyone associated with James, she determined there and then to find out. Anyone with a voice like that was someone she needed to know.

By Monday evening, Lizzie was in the depths of despair. Never mind dreams – her singing exam was over, and she'd messed up.

The examiner had been totally po-faced, and had been scribbling like crazy, which meant he had loads of things to criticise. She thought she'd done OK with the Vaughan Williams, and the Fauré *Chanson* was fine, but she'd totally blown the Handel aria and as for the Irish folk song – she was rubbish.

She'd never get Distinction now. So she might as well stop dreaming.

It had been a dumb idea anyway.

CHAPTER 8

'. . . a rational creature speaking the truth from her heart.'
(Jane Austen, *Pride and Prejudice*)

'YES, YES, YES!' LIZZIE PUNCHED THE AIR AND WAVED THE envelope above her head.

'She said yes! I got it! The first of October for six weeks – and maybe longer! Cool or what?'

'Lizzie, if I had the slightest idea what you're talking about,' her father observed, draining the dregs of his coffee before leaving for work on Thursday morning. (Three days doing the sights of London and Stratford on Avon with Drew had given Harry a sudden urge to attend to overdue paperwork at the office.)

'A placement with Madeleine LeFevre,' Lizzie cried. 'At her music centre in France – doing singing therapy. Me!'

'Darling, that's wonderful news,' Harry replied. 'I knew you were trying to get work experience at a concert hall or something, but you never mentioned you were applying for a placement abroad.'

'I only found out about it when we were on the choir trip,' Lizzie explained, thrusting the letter into her mother's hands as she came into the kitchen. 'There was a guy from the LeFevre Centre at one of our concerts and he was going on about student placements. You must have read about the place, Dad?'

'Well, no, I —'

'It's famous all over the world for getting through to kids with brain injuries and autism and stuff, through music therapy and singing.'

She gave him a hug.

'This guy said that one of their placement students had dropped out and they were re-advertising. I thought I'd go for it. I never dreamed I'd get it. And it's not conditional on my exam results – so I can go anyway!'

'Well,' her mother said, scanning the letter and looking as pleased as if she'd achieved it all herself, 'that'll be something to tell them all at the mast meeting tonight, won't it? If I hear one more word from that Helen Bradbury-Wells about how her daughter's going to be on the front cover of *Tatler* . . .'

'Mum, never mind her, can't you just be pleased for me?'

'What? Of course I'm pleased. I'm ecstatic. Just wait till I tell . . . Lizzie? Lizzie where are you going?'

'France?' Drew exclaimed later that morning after Lizzie, still on a high from her good news, had volunteered to take him to Sulgrave Manor for one of their Living History days. 'Wow – that's great.'

'Yes,' Lizzie admitted, biting her lip as she nervously negotiated a roundabout. 'There must have been loads of applications.'

'No, no, I mean you and me in France at the same time,' Drew countered.

'France is a very big country,' Lizzie said hastily. 'I mean, I'll be down at Figeac. It's a town in the south-west.'

'I don't believe it! The south-west? That can't be far from Balaguier, which is where I'll be working,' Drew said. 'Isn't that thrilling?'

Lizzie, brought up not to tell lies unless absolutely necessary, said nothing.

'Say,' Drew continued undaunted, 'on my days off we could meet up and have ourselves a good time.'

'Mmm,' Lizzie murmured non-comittally, since good times and Drew were worlds apart. 'So come on, tell me – what do you know about the Washington family and Sulgrave Manor?'

As she had hoped, Drew was so taken up with expounding his knowledge of Anglo-American history ('I don't like to brag, but I majored in history and my tutor said he'd never seen a brain as retentive as mine') that the subject of France was forgotten.

Lizzie made a mental note not to raise it again.

Whatever faults Drew had, Lizzie had to admit he was very enthusiastic. He bounded round the manor like a puppy on speed, gasping with delight at the Tudor kitchen with its spit and bread oven, ooh-ed and aah-ed over the herb garden and listened avidly to the talk of Remedies of Bygone Days, even engaging the guide in an in-depth conversation as to whether calendula would cure his athlete's foot.

He bought her what he called 'one of your awesome

English afternoon teatimes' in the Buttery café, and insisted on taking her photograph in a dozen different locations to email to the folks back home.

And then he suggested a walk in the woods.

'So come on, Lizzie, tell me all about yourself,' Drew urged as he groped for her hand, and Lizzie tried equally determinedly to avoid it. 'I know Jane's doing sociology, and Meredith's set on saving the planet – but what floats your boat?'

'Music,' Lizzie replied at once. 'Singing, mainly.'

'Oh yes, of course – you were quite the best in the church choir on Sunday. That solo verse you had – brilliant! I was transported.'

I wish, thought Lizzie.

'And, of course, I am used to an exceptionally high standard of choral singing at Willow Grove Congregational. So do you want to be a singer?'

'I don't know what I want to do yet,' Lizzie replied hastily. She knew it was a lie, but she had a feeling that if she were to verbalise her dream to Drew, the whole family would know about it within a day, and then the pressure would really be on.

'But school? You're going in October?'

Lizzie shook her head.

'I'm taking a gap year,' she told him, sidestepping quickly to avoid Drew's arm which was hovering dangerously near her right shoulder. 'What I'd really like is to do so well at the Centre in September that Madame LeFevre keeps me on for the rest of the year. That would be so cool.'

'Wouldn't that just be the most perfect thing?' Drew breathed, edging closer to Lizzie. 'Us together in France – what could be better?'

Root-canal work by a blind dentist, Lizzie thought, but refrained from commenting and merely smiled. She should have stuck to her promise and kept her mouth shut.

'The moment I saw you, I just knew,' Drew went on. 'And you did too, didn't you?'

'Knew what?' Lizzie asked cautiously.

'That spark between us – you felt it, surely? No, don't deny it. I just know you did. Oh Lizzie, you are so gorge—'

'Drew!' Lizzie shouted as he began pulling her towards him. 'Get off me! Like now!'

'All I'm saying is don't ever expect me to go anywhere with Drew on my own,' Lizzie declared that evening, after Harry had taken their visitor off to the County Cricket Ground to watch the Twenty20 match and she and Jane were getting ready to go to the cinema. 'God, his hands had a life of their own.'

'Well, I bet he got the message,' Jane said with a smile.

'You think?' Lizzie retorted. 'I doubt it – he tried to pretend I was being coy. Kept winking at me and making suggestive remarks all the way home. At least on Saturday there'll be a crowd of us and someone else can hang out with him.'

She turned to Meredith, who was attempting to ram her sleeping bag into its bag in preparation for her trip the following day.

'Pity you won't be around to come along,' she teased. 'You seem to get on with him OK.'

'I think he's quite a troubled soul,' Meredith said solemnly. 'And anyway, he listens to me. Which is more than can be said for the rest of you.'

'Well, of course, you could always invite him along to drain ditches or whatever it is you're going to do.'

'I could, couldn't I?' Meredith said thoughtfully. 'Only all the places are full, and besides, it's for under twenty-ones and —'

'Meredith? It was a joke.'

Her sister yanked the drawstring of the bag and glared at Lizzie. 'Everything I do is a joke to you, isn't it?' she retorted. 'But don't worry about it – the people who matter take me seriously.' She eyed them smugly. 'I just heard – the *Chronicle* want me to do a weekly piece for teenagers all about how to make their families more aware of conservation issues. They want it to be really hard hitting.'

'You'd be good at that,' Jane said encouragingly, shooting Lizzie a warning glance.

'Trouble is, they want it to be funny too,' Meredith said. 'And conservation is a really serious matter.'

'Ah,' said Lizzie. 'I can see that would be tricky. Hey, is that my phone?'

She fumbled in the pocket of her shorts.

Text message, read her phone.

She punched the Read button.

Just 2 say Hi 2 sum1 very sexy! Drew xxx

Lizzie hurled the phone at Jane, who read the message and exploded into giggles.

'How the hell did he get my number?' she stormed.

'Dad gave him all our numbers the day he arrived,' Jane said. 'He thought they might come in handy in an emergency.'

'Thanks, Dad,' muttered Lizzie. 'Jane, how am I going to stop this creep coming on to me?'

'Well,' Jane mused, 'you could pray that he finds someone else. Although that's hardly going to happen within the next two weeks.'

'Jane, you are a star! Of course – it's obvious. They're made for one another.'

She snatched her phone and punched in a number.

'Come on, come on . . . oh, hi Emily! It's me, Lizzie. Say, how do you fancy a day at the races on Saturday? What? Oh, loads of people – and guys too. Yes, available ones. You will? Cool!'

She tossed the phone aside and grinned at Jane.

'Lizzie, Em's your friend,' Jane said. 'You can't honestly expect she'd fancy Drew?'

'Jane, Emily's desperate to have a guy. I'm desperate to get him off my back. What's to argue about?'

In the event, getting rid of Drew turned out to be rather more difficult than Lizzie had hoped. Since James was driving Caroline, Charlie and Jane in his Ferrari, and Denny had invited the twins to take the last two places in the college minibus, it was left to Lizzie to borrow her mum's Polo on Saturday morning and take Emily and Drew to Brighton. Trying to keep up with James on the motorway was a total impossibility in the Polo. Added to which, her nervousness, combined with the unceasing flow of conversation from Drew as he filled Emily in on his complete life history, job prospects and the fact that this quaint little race meeting would be nothing compared to the Kentucky Derby where his mom had taken a box, meant that when she finally parked up and found the Members' enclosure, she was feeling more than a little frazzled.

'Hey, Lizzie, where've you been? We arrived ages ago!' Lydia, a glass of what Lizzie hoped was lemonade in one hand, bounced over to them.

'Hi Emily, hi Drew, isn't this the coolest thing?' She looked, Lizzie had to admit, a million dollars and way more than her fifteen years. Wearing a scarlet mini-dress and a funky cloche hat, from which peeped huge fake tiger's eye earrings, she looked like a cover girl for *Teen Vogue* rather than a kid who hadn't yet taken her GCSEs. And just for a moment, Lizzie envied her.

'Come on,' Lydia urged. 'We're all in the Champagne bar. Posh or what?' She grabbed Lizzie's hand. 'Well, not all of us, actually, because Denny and the guys are helping to set up the stand, but they'll be along in a bit. Denny's cousin is with them – he's called George and he's really fit. And guess what? I think Katie's actually managing to pull! Like how bizarre is that?'

Lizzie opened her mouth to reply, but Lydia was in full flood as they pushed their way through the clusters of drinkers outside the bar.

'Amber and Tim are here too – you know I told you Amber's keen on Tim? Well, she is and anyway, Tim's bought his mate Ben along and he sat next to Katie in the minibus, and she was going all pink, you know like she does when she's shy, which is always, of course, but then . . .'

She babbled on, regardless of the fact that Lizzie couldn't hear a word she was saying over the noise of the bar, which was packed with racegoers, some poring over their race cards and perusing the *Racing Post*, some watching the odds on the overhead screens and others queuing for expensively priced seafood.

They elbowed their way through to the far corner, Drew managing en route to blunder into one woman and send her plate of prawns crashing to the floor before standing on someone's foot, causing them to spill their champagne down his trouser leg.

'You'd better help him sort it out,' Lizzie muttered to Emily, shoving her eagerly in his direction as he flapped about with a handkerchief. 'Look after him, will you? He's not fit to be let out on his own.' (Lizzie had read enough psychology books to know that Emily loved being needed, and estimated that with a bit of luck she would be glued to Drew's side for the rest of the day.)

'I owe you an apology.'

Lizzie turned as someone tapped her on the shoulder. To her surprise, James, looking like one of the society guys in the social pages of *Tatler* with his straw trilby and navy blazer and appearing more relaxed than she'd ever seen him, took her arm, leading her towards the bar where a couple of spare stools had become vacant.

'I should have driven more slowly,' he admitted. 'I didn't realise you'd only just passed your test and by the time Jane mentioned it, I'd completely lost you. Sorry.'

For a moment, Lizzie was speechless. When he smiled, James looked far less arrogant and he did appear genuinely concerned.

'That's OK,' she murmured.

'Now then, I guess you're not used to being in places like this,' James went on, pausing to let a stout guy balancing a plate of lobster salad edge past him. '"The Members", I mean. There's an etiquette in these places; bit archaic but —'

'But totally beyond a state-school kid to cope with, is that what you mean?' Lizzie snapped, silently admonishing herself for ever thinking the guy could change.

'Oh, for God's sake,' James retorted, perching on a stool. 'Do you only have one line of repartee? Is it beyond you to come up with something new? I don't give a damn how much you argue with me, but you are getting to be rather boring!'

'Not half as boring as your patronising attitude,' Lizzie countered, noting with relief that Emily had managed to move Drew away from his somewhat irate victims. 'So how about you treat me like I've got a brain, and I overlook the fact that you are so out of touch with reality as to be unreal?'

To her surprise, James burst out laughing. 'Better!' he replied. 'Much better. There's hope for you — Oh dear! That was patronising, I guess?'

Despite herself, Lizzie smiled.

'I've heard you say worse,' she replied. 'So – if I promise not to swear, strip off or create a scene unworthy of such elevated company, why don't you tell me more about your sister? That CD —'

'Not now,' James said. 'Not here. OK?'

It was the look of raw emotion on his face that stopped Lizzie from pressing him further.

'So – how about you? I know you live in France, but . . .'

'Not full time – that's my aunt's place. And a whole other story. My home – the place my father grew up – is in Braemar. That's in Scotland.'

'No! You don't say? And me with my crap education thought it was in Africa.'

James grinned and held his hands up in mock surrender.

'And are you at uni in Scotland, then?' Lizzie asked.

James shook his head.

'I was at Oxford with Charlie,' he explained. 'But I'm about to start a Masters in International Human Rights Law at Birkbeck College in London.'

'Wow,' Lizzie began, and then decided to change the subject. No way did she want to look even mildly impressed. Or surprised that James Darcy was even vaguely interested in human rights.

'And how about your aunt's horse? Is that an OK subject?'

'He's called The Bog Hurdler and he runs in the 2.45 – that's the second race. Can't see him doing much, though; he's used to a mile and this is a mile and two furlongs. He won't stay, the trainer's already said that, but when my aunt makes her mind up about something, nothing will shift her.'

'So that's where you get it from,' Lizzie observed, softening her remark with a wry grin. 'Family characteristic!'

'I'm not always stubborn,' he replied, his voice husky. 'Honestly. And actually, I was wondering whether —'

'Come on, you two, we're going to the paddock to size up the runners for the first race!' Charlie appeared at their side, flapping a race card in their faces. 'Denny and the guys are manning the stand till the second race – they'll join us then. One of the ex-students from Longbourn is riding a horse called Stuck Fast. Not a very auspicious name, I guess!'

'So,' Jane whispered to Lizzie as they followed the guys out of the bar and past the grandstand to the paddock, 'what's with the change of heart? I saw you flirting with James.'

'What are you on? I was not flirting!' Lizzie exclaimed.

'Well, you weren't objecting to being chatted up, were you now?'

'Jane, are you insane? For one thing, he was not chatting me up. And I'll tell you something else: if James Darcy was the last guy left alive on the planet, I wouldn't give him a second look. I was just being polite. For your sake. Because he's a friend of Charlie's.'

'Lizzie Bennet,' Jane replied, 'you are a hopeless liar.'

CHAPTER 9

'A man of . . . fine countenance, a good figure and a very pleasing address.'
(Jane Austen, *Pride and Prejudice*)

'HOW DO YOU TELL WHICH HORSE IS LIKELY TO WIN?' Lizzie mused, leaning against the white fence around the paddock as the horses paraded before the start of the first race.

'Of course, I keep forgetting you're a bit out of your depth here, aren't you?' Caroline remarked coolly. 'It's far too complicated to explain right now, but I reckon number four – Twist 'n' Shout – will romp home. Strong withers, prancing gait, isn't that right, James?'

'Nonsense,' James objected. 'Hook, Line and Sinker will make mincemeat of the rest of the field. Loves hard going, performs over the distance and the pedigree is top notch. I know the trainer and he reckons . . .'

Lizzie drifted off, preferring to people-watch and enjoy the combined effects of sunshine and fresh air than to listen to pretentious conversation.

To her alarm, she saw Drew heading determinedly towards her – and there was no sign of Emily.

'Lizzie, there you are,' he said. 'Now come along, and tell me which horse to back.'

'I don't know anything about racing,' she said. 'You'd do better sticking a pin in the list of runners.'

'That's it!' Drew exclaimed. 'Look – there's a horse called Pinprick. It's an omen! Come along, let's get the money on fast.'

'I really don't want to waste money betting – um, where's Emily?'

'Oh don't you worry about Emily – she's fine. She was talking to some of the kids from the college. Now do hurry – we must bet before the odds shorten. I know about these things, you see – my stepfather's a director of Leisure USA and when you've been to as many corporate events as I have . . .'

'Get on there, Pinprick!' Drew yelled. 'Move yourself, you crazy animal!'

Lizzie cringed as Drew's shouts became louder and louder. In view of his abandoned behaviour, she was relieved that he had taken so long to place his bet that they hadn't been able to get back to the Members' stand in time and were watching the race from the rails, well away from the others.

'Yes, yes, yes!'

A roar went up from the crowd as Pinprick passed the post a neck ahead of Hook, Line and Sinker.

Drew turned to Lizzie, lifted her off her feet and swung her round in excitement. For an instant, she laughed, more from delight that James had been proved wrong than from anything else.

And then he kissed her. On the lips. And despite her frantic wriggling, for far, far too long.

'You are so out of order!' she shouted, when she had finally managed a swift dig in his stomach with her elbow and a carefully aimed kick to his ankle.

'But Lizzie . . .' he began.

'Don't you "but Lizzie" me,' she snapped, wiping her lips with the back of her hand in disgust. 'Who do you think you are? I would have thought you'd got the message by now – *I don't fancy you!*'

She turned and began walking swiftly back towards the Members' grandstand, embarrassingly aware of titters from the surrounding crowd.

'You don't?' Drew called after her. 'So how come you were so eager to tell me all about going to France? Like it was a coincidence that you chose to be somewhere you knew I'd be?'

'I did what? You're mad!' she shouted. 'I hadn't even met you when I applied for the placement and believe me, if I had, I'd have chosen any country on earth but where you'd be!'

'Well, thank you so much,' Drew snapped back. 'You know, my mom warned me about your family before I came. She said that if the kids were anything like the parents, social climbers from a rundown backwater, totally out for themselves and —'

'Just stop right there,' Lizzie said, wheeling round to face him. 'No one, ever, talks about my family like that. Now I know you're our guest and I won't mention this to anyone. Unless . . .' She took a deep breath. '. . . you ever put a foot out of line with me again. In which case, I won't be responsible.'

She paused as Emily came flying towards them.

'Oh my God, Lizzie, I won! Fifteen pounds. Isn't that cool?' She paused, eyeing Lizzie's scarlet cheeks. 'Hey, are you OK?'

Lizzie said nothing. Her heart was racing and she had a desperate urge to hit something hard.

'Emily,' Drew said at once, slipping his arm through hers. 'Why don't we go and get a drink to celebrate your win?'

'Well, OK, yeah – that'd be cool. Coming, Lizzie?'

Lizzie shook her head, still too angry to speak.

'Lizzie's having a bit of a bad day right now,' Drew drawled. 'I reckon we should just leave her alone. When you've had as much customer interface training as I have . . .'

It wasn't until Lizzie had finished counting from a hundred in French backwards, that she felt calm enough to rejoin the others.

'You need one of these. They don't let just anyone in.' James handed Lizzie a badge allowing her to go into the paddock for the second race, along with the owners and trainers. 'I'm just going over to have a chat with the trainer and the jockey. Catch you in a minute.'

'Don't walk behind any horses and remember they'll be fizzed up, so don't get too close, OK?' Caroline warned.

As if I didn't know that, thought Lizzie. That girl is so totally up herself.

'Hey, Jamie, wait for me!' Caroline called as she

tottered off on four-inch slingbacks and slipped her arm through James's.

Lizzie was about to follow Charlie and Jane into the paddock, relieved that there was no sign of Drew or Emily, when there was an excited shriek from the rails.

'Lizzie! Wait for us!'

Lydia's shouts caused several heads to turn, and judging by the expressions on the faces of several of the owners and trainers, it wasn't in admiration.

Lizzie turned, ready to give her sister a steely stare. And caught her breath. Striding towards her, towering over Denny and the twins, was the sexiest, most gorgeous-looking guy she had ever seen. He had dark curly hair and a Mediterranean complexion, and as he caught Lizzie's furious expression, his face broke into a wide smile. And in that moment, Lizzie understood that all that stuff in the romantic novels her mother loved so much, about electricity coursing through your veins and knees trembling, wasn't, as she had always supposed, a load of badly written rubbish.

'Lizzie, meet George Wickham,' Denny said. 'He's my cousin back from a year in Australia, and he's staying with us for a while. George, this is Lizzie Bennet, Lydia and Katie's sister and over there, that's Jane and, of course, you know Charlie and Caro.'

He paused as Lydia shouted and beckoned furiously from the far side of the paddock.

'OK, OK, Lyddy, I'm coming!' he called. 'You two get to know one another for a minute, yeah?'

'Hello.' George's voice was deep and velvety and in that one word, he seemed able to pack a heap of meaning.

Lizzie smiled.

'Oh, that's better.'

'Pardon?'

'You looked really fierce a moment ago,' he said with a grin, as they began to move into the paddock. 'But now you're not so scary!'

Lizzie laughed. 'Sorry, it's my sister,' she said. 'She can be so over the top sometimes, it's embarrassing.'

'She's fun, though, isn't she?' George remarked. 'I mean, an hour in a minibus with her and a whole new universe opens up!'

'Tell me about it,' Lizzie replied. 'Oh, look, they're bringing the horses out – shall we go over and join the others?'

'I guess this is where we study form, as they say,' George said, pulling his race card from the pocket of his jacket.

'Mmm,' Lizzie murmured, conscious that her mind was very far from the horses and very much taken up with something far closer to hand.

'That one over there, that's the one I like the look of,' George remarked, pointing to a chestnut colt that was prancing about on his toes and tossing his head. 'What's it called? Oh yes, Trojan Prince.'

'Not the politically correct thing to say in this company,' giggled Lizzie. 'We're all supposed to be rooting for number ten. The Bog Hurdler. Over there – the jockey's just mounting, see?'

'Let's take a look.'

George strode over to where the others were all hovering around James and the trainer.

'So have you put money on this one, Denny?' George asked, tapping his cousin on the shoulder.

At the sound of his voice, James turned. And blanched. George's face turned scarlet. Their eyes met.

'You.' James's lips formed the word, but no sound came out of his mouth. George stared back, and then, without speaking, inclined his head ever so slightly and turned away.

The whole encounter took less than thirty seconds and Lizzie was pretty sure she was the only person who had noticed.

'Give it your all,' James said to the jockey, and without another word, slapped the horse once on the neck, turned and walked rapidly from the parade ring, the rest of the group tagging along behind.

'I think,' George said to Lizzie, 'it might be best if I watched the race from a distance.'

And before she could ask for an explanation, he raised his hand in a brief wave and disappeared swiftly into the crowd.

'What I don't understand,' Drew remarked to Charlie as the horses cantered up to the starting gates, 'is why James's horse is called The Bog Hurdler. I mean, it's a flat race horse, right?'

'Oh, it's an anagram of the name of his aunt's company,' Charlie explained. 'De Burgh Hotels – only she got one letter wrong – there's no "S" and —'

'*De Burgh Hotels?*' Drew exclaimed. 'You mean, James is the nephew of – oh, I don't believe it!'

He pushed past Lizzie and Emily and began edging along the row to where James, still grim-faced, was standing, binoculars raised to his eyes, watching as the horses were urged into the starting gates.

'James, you won't believe what I've just discovered. Your aunt is Katrina De Burgh!'

'Believe it or not, I was aware of that fact,' James replied.

'Yes, but you don't understand, it's the most amazing coincidence, because only last month . . .'

'Look, could you just be quiet, please,' James snapped. 'They're off!'

'Well, I guess third is better than nothing,' James remarked to Charlie at the end of the race. 'Even though he was five lengths behind the second. I'll text Auntie Kat.'

'And you can tell her,' Drew interjected eagerly, peering over his shoulder, 'that you've met me!'

'And this fact would be of interest to her?' James asked dryly.

'Oh yes, you see I'm her protégé, as you might say. I work for De Burgh Hotels and I'm on her fast-track management scheme. She's acquired a new hotel in France, well, a chateau actually.'

'*Acquired* is one way of putting it,' James muttered, punching a number into his phone.

'And I'll be going over there in just ten days' time,' Drew finished triumphantly.

'Dear God, no,' muttered James.

'I know, it's great, isn't it?' Drew blustered, obviously totally oblivious to the sarcasm of James's remark. 'She has great plans for it. And me!'

'Really?'

'Oh yes – now look, you and I must have a chat. You must tell me all about her – because, good as I am with people, it always helps to have the inside track. So come on, give me the low-down.'

'I make it a point never, ever to talk about my family to strangers. Now if you'll excuse me, I've got people to avoid.'

Lizzie spent the next half hour ignoring the racing and trying to find George. She was well aware that it was a crazy thing to do, to hunt down a guy she'd only spoken to for five minutes, but she'd never felt this way before. It was as if she'd downed two vodka tonics on an empty stomach – she was literally giddy with – well, not desire exactly, but . . . well, yes, she confessed to herself. Desire. He was absolutely gorgeous.

She hunted in all the bars, even leaving the Members' enclosure with its well-dressed punters and venturing into the Silver Ring, where the effects of cheap lager and holidaymakers driven from the beach by the recent oil slick were all too visible; she scoured the parade ring and the paddock, the Oyster bar and the Tote windows and then inspiration struck. The College stand!

She followed the signs to the *Fun day activities and shopping village*, past the face painters, the hobby horse races and the stalls selling riding gear and shooting sticks, and had just caught sight of the banner announcing *Longbourn College of Equine Studies – Galloping into the Future* when she saw something that stopped her dead in her tracks.

Jane was sitting on a bench, looking up into the face

of a sandy-haired guy, whose arm was gently caressing her neck. As Lizzie watched, their lips met.

'Bless,' she thought. 'She and Charlie really are getting it together.'

And then the guy looked up.

It wasn't Charlie.

It was Simon.

'Are you OK? Jane, don't cry.'

'I should never have done that,' Jane sobbed.

'Oh yes, you should.'

'It was just – well, he was trying to say that I was overreacting, and couldn't we get together again, and that business with the chat room had just been a joke, and you know what, Lizzie . . .'

'For a moment you believed him?'

Her sister nodded.

'I should never have come,' she said. 'That job he got – on the local paper, yeah? Well, he was here doing a piece about the races – he's applied for a job on *Sporting Life* and wants loads of good stuff in his portfolio.'

'Never mind all that,' Lizzie interrupted. 'The main thing is you got rid of the creep. Honestly, when I spotted you kissing, I nearly had kittens, but then when you slapped him – well, I wanted to cheer!'

'But I shouldn't have done it,' Jane protested. 'I can't believe I was that vicious.'

'I can't believe he came on to you like that – kissing you, after all he's put you through. Slime bag.'

A sudden thought struck her.

'And where's Charlie? Why are you on your own?'

Jane bit her lip and looked mildly embarrassed.

'I – er – spotted Simon, and I told Charlie I needed the loo. Don't look at me like that – I just wanted closure with Simon.'

'Well, you've got it,' Lizzie said firmly. 'And I suggest that you get back to Charlie right now. He's worth a dozen Simons.'

She paused, the memory that had been on her mind for the past ten minutes refusing to go away.

'You do know, don't you, that you mistook James for Simon when you were in the hospital? James was in the doorway and you called him Si and said you loved him.'

'I guess I have to take your word for it – everything was a bit of a blur.'

'You really are over Simon? You don't actually love that loser? I mean, if you're not . . .'

'Believe me, after today – he can go fry in oil. There's only one guy I want.'

'At last! She admits it!' Lizzie laughed. 'So what are you doing hanging about with me? Go get him!'

'Oh. Hi.' Lizzie tried hard to make it sound as if George Wickham was the last person she'd expected to see sprawled out on the grass fiddling with his BlackBerry beside the College stand. 'I was just – er . . .'

She was saved from inventing a lie by George jumping to his feet, dusting grass off his trousers and looking at her intently.

'You must have thought I was a real jerk, dashing off like that,' he began. 'It was so rude of me. So – what do you say I buy you a drink to make up for it?'

'That would be great,' Lizzie replied and then cringed inwardly for sounding so eager.

'Not the Champagne bar, though,' George went on. 'Don't think I'd be welcome there right now. How about we slum it a bit and amble down to the start with a Pimm's? Plastic glasses, I'm afraid, but it's the drink that matters!'

'Sure,' Lizzie nodded. 'That would be cool.'

As they queued at the marquee for their drinks, George turned to her.

'Have you – um – known James Darcy for long?'

Lizzie shook her head. 'Only a couple of weeks,' she said.

'I've known him all my life,' George told her.

'You have? But I thought – I mean . . .'

'I guess you spotted the fact that he wasn't exactly over the moon to see me,' George said.

'I did notice, yes,' Lizzie admitted.

'I guess you and he are pretty good friends, yeah?'

'You must be joking!' Lizzie laughed. 'I do have a little taste. James is the most arrogant, pompous git I've ever . . .'

George laughed. 'I don't think the county set would agree with you there. I hear that he's one of the in crowd who gets invited to all the best parties, shoots on the Balmoral estate, hunts in France . . . the works.'

He pulled a face and then smiled at her. 'But I'm with you – I think he's detestable. He ruined my life – or at least, made a damn good attempt to.'

'He did what?' Lizzie gasped, as they began strolling past the five furlong marker and on towards the start.

'It's a long story,' George said. 'And I'm sure you don't want to hear it.'

'No, please, I do,' Lizzie urged.

'OK, then. My father and his father – Alexander Darcy – were really close friends. They played for the local cricket team, belonged to the same golf club and were both mad about vintage cars.' He paused. 'You know, of course, that James's dad was headmaster of Heddingfield?'

'Heddingfield?' Lizzie gasped. 'Isn't that the posh boarding school that loads of celebs send their kids to?'

'Uh-huh,' George nodded. 'And a few minor royals. My father was head groundsman there and Alexander was my godfather. My mum died when I was really little and, to be honest, James's dad was the one who got my father through it.'

He took a swig of his drink.

'He understood how my father was feeling – Mrs Darcy had been killed in a car crash the year before, when James was three. So he knew what it was like to bring kids up on your own. Sorry, I'm boring you,' he said, as he watched the horses canter up to the start for the fourth race. 'I'll shut up and we'll watch the race.'

'No, please, go on,' Lizzie said.

'OK, but let's sit.' He gestured to a white bench near the rails and they sat down.

'James and I used to play together in the holidays – they had a grace and favour house in the school grounds as well as their home in Scotland; I lived in the village with Dad,' George told her. 'I was clever – I mean, I know that sounds conceited, but it's a fact – and the local comprehensive was rubbish – I was bored stiff and Mr Darcy knew it. So guess what? When I was thirteen,

Mr Darcy engineered me a full scholarship to Heddingfield. I could never have gone otherwise – I mean, it was beyond our wildest dreams.'

'So how come . . .?' Lizzie began.

'How come it all went sour?' George asked. 'Within a couple of terms of starting at the school, James took against me. Don't ask me why, but he did. I was popular – I had lots of girlfriends and he didn't. Could have been that, I guess – it's a co-ed school, you know, and if a guy doesn't have a girl, well he's kinda out of things.'

'Well, I guess you'd have to be pretty desperate to go out with a guy like James,' Lizzie suggested. Whereas you, she added silently in her head, are something else.

George shrugged.

'Anyway, Mr Darcy was really good to me – he got me extra tuition in subjects that state schools don't cover – Latin and stuff; he paid for some of the equipment I needed and he told me that he was pretty sure I'd make Cambridge if I worked hard.'

'That's brilliant – and did you?' Lizzie asked.

'Work hard? Sure. Get to Cambridge? Thanks to James, no, I didn't,' he said abruptly, downing the rest of his drink and chucking the plastic cup into the nearest bin. 'I was expelled six months before taking my A-levels.'

'Expelled? What did you do?'

'I made one foolish mistake,' he replied, a touch of bitterness in his voice. 'I tried to help James's sister.'

Lizzie's eyes widened.

'His sister? Jenna?'

'You know her?' George sounded anxious.

'Never met her,' Lizzie said. 'But I heard her singing on a CD . . .'

'Oh yeah,' George nodded. 'Lovely voice – she sang in the school choir, solos and everything. Sounds like an angel, doesn't she? It's a pity she's turned into such a conniving, manipulative little cow.'

'But you said you were helping her?' Lizzie asked.

'She was a cute kid when she was younger, but then at Heddingfield, she got in with a bad lot – even the best public schools have them, although they don't like to admit it. By the time she was fourteen, she was dabbling in drugs.'

'Oh God!' Lizzie gasped.

'I found out.' George sighed. 'She had a crush on me, you see. She would follow me around, send me little notes, and I thought if she'd listen to anyone it would be me. But then one day . . .' He took a deep breath. 'I guess she thought it was clever and it would make her look sophisticated – she offered me some cocaine.'

'Dumb kid! What did you do? Tell her father, obviously?'

George shook his head. 'Mr Darcy had had his first heart attack the month before, and news like that could have killed him. Or at least, that's what I thought at the time. In the event, he died anyway.'

For a moment, Lizzie felt a huge wave of sorrow for James. No mum, and now no father – that was hard. 'Poor James.' The words were out before she realised.

George nodded curtly.

'Three years ago, when I was in the second year of Sixth Form, Mr Darcy died. Another massive heart attack on the morning of Open Day. Awful.' He shook his head, deep in memories.

'Well, of course, once he was dead and I realised that Jenna was still into substances – I had to tell someone. I told James. That was my big mistake.'

'He didn't believe you?'

'I thought he did. I told him I thought it was grief over her father's death that had pushed her into it. I didn't let on how long it had been going on. And he said he'd deal with it. Thanked me, even, for going to him. Next thing I know I'm up before the school governors and the deputy head and being expelled.'

'But . . .'

'He framed me. I guess I can't blame him.'

'Of course you can bloody blame him,' Lizzie retorted. 'That's the most awful thing to do – but how? How did he do it?'

'I was told that a wrap of cocaine had been found in my room,' George said. 'I thought I'd flushed all the stuff I took off Jenna down the loo but I suppose I could have missed one.'

'So you told them? Said it like it was?'

'You don't know how the system works with these upper-class inbreds,' George snapped, and then checked himself. 'Sorry, that was uncalled-for. It's just – well, Jenna swore black was white that I'd tried to get her hooked on the stuff. She even said I'd come on to her and snogged her – and yes, I hugged her once when she was crying because she felt so awful after snorting the stuff. See, it was no use. No one was going to believe me.'

'I believe you,' Lizzie said.

'Thank you.' George's smile lit up his whole face. 'I know we've only just met, but that means a lot.'

His fingers brushed hers and her whole body tingled.

'Come on,' he said suddenly, his tone of voice lightening. 'Let's head back. I fancy one of those swish crab sandwiches.'

'But what if James . . .'

'He may want to avoid me, and that's up to him,' George said. 'I'm not going to stop doing what I want just to keep him happy. Too many people have done that for too long.'

'Good for you,' Lizzie said. 'But what I don't get is how come Charlie and Caroline can be friends with a guy who can behave like that?'

'Oh, don't get me wrong, James can be absolutely great with people he approves of – his own set, you know? The two homes, three cars brigade, I call them. But with people who try to better themselves, well, that's different. He used to slag off my mates from the comprehensive – said he didn't know why I kept in touch with them.'

'I can believe that,' Lizzie replied. 'He thinks I'm the pits because I went to Meryton Academy. You must tell Charlie —'

'No way. I am not the kind of person to do that,' George said, quickening his pace. 'In fact you're the first to know the whole truth.'

'Well, I'll tell them,' she insisted. 'I mean, seeing the way they hang on his every word . . .'

'Please. Don't.'

'Why not?'

'James was only trying to protect his sister, I guess. And – well, his father was like a dad to me,' he said. 'Before he died, when I visited him in hospital, he asked me always to be a mate to his kids. "Friends," he said, "are what holds lives together." Well, right now, they won't let me, but one day . . .' His voice broke. 'One day, please God, they'll come round and everything can be sorted and forgiven.'

'You are one amazing guy,' Lizzie breathed. 'I could never be that tolerant.'

'I believe in live and let live,' George smiled. 'And hey – life's good now. I took a year out, travelling in Australia – I have to be on the go, I can't just sit around feeling sorry for myself, you see. I worked as a lifeguard on Bondi Beach for a bit, learned survival skills in the bush, did a bit of sailing. And now . . . well, I'm staying with Denny for a while and then, who knows what the future holds?'

He smiled at Lizzie and her heart missed a beat.

'I just have a feeling that whatever it is, it's going to be very good.'

'Come off it, Jane, how could he have made it up?'

All day, Lizzie's mind had been full of what George had told her. She hadn't seen him after their talk, but not seeing him didn't mean her mind was not full of him. Full of everything he had told her, and full of how he looked, how he sounded, how his eyes reflected all his emotions – sadness, hurt, regret. And she couldn't help wondering: did he fancy her? Just a little bit?

It wasn't until late that evening that she had the chance to offload on Jane. Knowing how her sister always defended the underdog, she had expected her to explode with anger at the first mention of James Darcy's behaviour. Instead, her sister simply sat there on the end of her bed, looking at Lizzie as if she was crazy and shaking her head in disbelief.

'I just don't believe it,' Jane insisted.

'Why not? Why would George lie?'

'For one thing, Charlie would never be taken in by a guy who was that devious – and he and James have been really close mates all the way through uni.'

'So?' Lizzie demanded. 'Charlie wasn't at school with him, and George was. So which one is more likely to know the truth?'

For a moment, Jane hesitated, but only for a moment.

'Look, Lizzie, people don't get expelled on a whim,' she reasoned. 'Especially from a high profile place like Heddingfield. If George was as innocent as he's led you to believe . . .'

'He is, Jane, I know he is,' Lizzie said. 'It was just that he couldn't prove it. I mean, he didn't hide anything, he told me every detail – and he's not even bearing a grudge like I would in his position.'

'Know what?' Jane smiled. 'I reckon you fancy him.'

Lizzie nibbled on her thumbnail.

'I – er – well, yes, I do a bit. I mean, he's so – well, just lovely. There's no side to him – what you see is what you get.'

'How can you say that?' Jane demanded. 'I mean you only met eight hours ago – and for all of ten minutes!'

'I just know,' Lizzie replied. 'When it comes to people, I always trust my intuition. And I know that George Wickham is a whole heap better than James Darcy could ever hope to be.'

CHAPTER 10

'A lady's imagination is very rapid; it jumps from admiration to love . . . in a moment.'
(Jane Austen, *Pride and Prejudice*)

'YOU ARE JOKING? EMILY – ARE YOU SAYING DREW KISSED you?'

Lizzie stared at Emily as she climbed into the passenger seat beside her later, the day before her party.

'Is that so amazing?' Emily challenged. 'Am I that hideous?'

'Don't be silly,' Lizzie retorted. 'I'm just surprised, that's all.'

She thought it best not to mention her episode at the races.

'Well, it was only a quick kiss,' Emily admitted. 'But he asked if I had a boyfriend, and when I said no, he said he just knew that was all about to change.'

For a moment the power of speech failed Lizzie totally and she felt hugely guilty.

'Emily, I'm so sorry,' she began. 'I mean, I know I pushed you and Drew together and I was really grateful when you took him over to Cambridge for the day, but —'

'So you're saying you want him now, is that it?' Emily broke in. 'Well, fine, if you do, fight me for him. Because I'm sick of always being the one who can't get a guy and I reckon I could pull him big time.'

'Fine, but —'

'But nothing. I know what you'd do – pull him, and then in a few months, drop him, like you did with Toby. I'm not like that. I want a guy and I want one for keeps. And tomorrow, at my party, I'm going to go for it, OK? And if you don't like it —'

'Emily, it's fine. OK. You go for it. Drew Collins is the last person on earth I want.'

'So what are you making the fuss about?'

'I'm not – I'm just – well, he's not exactly . . .'

'Good enough for you? I doubt the person exists who would suit you.' Had it not been for the teasing note in Emily's voice, Lizzie could have taken offence, but her friend nudged her and grinned.

'If you really like Drew, then bring it on,' Lizzie said.

'I don't know him well enough to like him or not like him,' Emily replied, her honesty taking Lizzie by surprise. 'But I don't get guys easily and this one seems to be available. Like, I am so not going to pass up on that.'

She snapped her seat belt into place, and turned to Lizzie. 'Now, are you going to come and help me choose a totally sexy outfit or not?'

'You've already got three new dresses.' Lizzie laughed.

'Yeah, I know,' Emily grinned. 'But now I need a pulling dress. Come on!'

The Lucases had really pushed the boat out for Emily's

eighteenth. Mr Lucas had recently sold the family business, Lucas Lighting ('shedding light in your darkest corners') to a national chain of furniture stores for a massive amount of money and clearly was not averse to spending a great deal of it entertaining everyone he knew.

He had hired the whole of Longbourn Country Club for a dinner for a hundred and twenty guests, including all the Bingleys and the Bennets and a number of Mr Lucas's business colleagues. A huge marquee had been erected in the grounds to which another hundred people had been invited for dancing to a live band. Emily had invited absolutely everyone she knew and her sister Maria had been only too willing to make up the numbers with her mates – and the club's bistro had been transformed into a 1950s-style American ice-cream parlour and soda fountain.

The driveway to the club was illuminated by Chinese lanterns swinging on bamboo poles and each dinner guest found a white tea light candle in a tiny replica lantern at their place.

From the moment the Bennets arrived, Lizzie had been scanning the room, hoping to catch sight of George. She knew Emily had invited him – she'd made sure of that during the long day spent in a dozen fitting rooms while her friend tried to find the definitive dress for seduction. (Lizzie had finally persuaded her to buy a gorgeous floaty aquamarine and seaweed-green dress and a pair of strappy metallic sandals, had spent two hours highlighting her hair for her and now, looking at the result, she had to admit that the time hadn't been wasted.)

'Hi, Lizzie, how you doing?' She turned to see Denny,

for once without Lydia at his side. 'Got a message from George – he can't come tonight.'

Her heart sank like lead. She'd blown a load of cash on a slinky black dress that was rather more revealing than her usual choice and now . . .

'Why?'

'He's had to go to London,' Denny said. 'One of his mates has arrived from Oz and has got himself into a bit of a mess – got mugged first day and has no cash. George felt he had to go and help him out.'

He lowered his voice, glancing across the room. 'Although between you and me, I don't think he'd have dashed off so fast if a certain person hadn't been invited to the party.'

Lizzie followed his gaze. James was standing staring intently at her. Catching her eye, he turned and walked to the other side of the room.

'Anyway,' Denny went on, 'he says he's gutted to be missing it and that he would have phoned you, but he doesn't have your number. He asked me to give you his.'

He handed her a piece of paper.

'Thank you,' she replied, her heart lifting a little. At least he wanted her to make contact. And that had to be good.

'James keeps looking at you!' Emily sidled up to Lizzie as the guests were making their way to their tables for the meal. 'I think he fancies you.'

'For God's sake, Emily, you're obsessed!' Lizzie retorted. 'There's only one person on the planet that James fancies and that's himself. You know what I told you.'

'About him and George thingy – where is George, by the way? I invited him like you asked me to. Why isn't he here?'

'Because he can't bear to be in the same room as James,' Lizzie said. 'And if it wasn't for you being my best friend, I wouldn't either.'

'Well, you are, so please, can you force a smile?' Emily asked. 'By the way, I bet Jane'll miss Charlie after tomorrow. Pity she's not going.'

'Going where?'

'To Tuscany, silly,' Emily replied. 'Didn't she tell you? The Bingleys go every August for about six weeks, usually. They'd be there by now if it wasn't for Charlie's dad being – well, you know.'

'No, I don't – I mean, I know he's been ill.'

'Nervous breakdown, very hush hush,' Emily whispered.

'Why? What's to be ashamed of?'

'Well, you know, people thinking he's loopy.'

'God, that is so stupid.'

'Yes, well, anyway – they've got this huge villa and Caroline and Charlie always take friends. I reckon Jane should really go for it tonight, come on so strong that Charlie won't want to leave her behind. That way she gets a freebie holiday.'

'Emily, what planet are you on? They only met three weeks ago.'

'So? You said ages ago that she needed something to take her mind off that jerk that two-timed her. Well. I reckon Charlie's it. Come on, we've got to sit down now. I've put myself next to Drew – hope you don't mind.'

'Mind? I'm over the moon,' Lizzie laughed. 'Rather you than me.'

'Lizzie, come and dance.'

James held out his hand, his eyes locked on hers.

'I . . .' She was about to refuse, but then something like anger stirred inside her and she took his hand. Why should she avoid confronting the guy?

For a while they didn't speak, the volume of the music and the crush on the dance floor in the marquee making conversation virtually impossible. Besides, Lizzie wasn't sure how to raise the subject of George. Luckily, James gave her the perfect opportunity.

'Did you enjoy the races?' he asked as the band moved off for their break and the disco DJ took over. 'Your sister said you'd never been before.'

'It was fun,' she acknowledged. 'Meeting new people is always good.'

She held his eye and he was the first to look away.

'George,' he muttered.

'Yes, George. Such a friendly guy.'

'Oh, sure.' James gave a short laugh. 'He makes friends easily enough; pity he's not so good at keeping them.'

'That's rich coming from you,' she retorted, amazed at his audacity. 'From what I gather, you've hardly been a friend to him. Ruined his life, more like.'

'Listen, I don't know what he's told you, but . . . oh, what's the point?'

He turned away abruptly, just as Lizzie's mother came scuttling over to her.

'There you are, I've been looking for you all over,' she

began, grabbing Lizzie's arm. 'Did you know the Bingleys have a house in Italy?'

'Yes, Emily told me,' Lizzie replied. 'Mum, I'm busy and —'

'And Jane thinks – well, she says she doesn't, but you know Jane, always timid and hanging back – anyway, I think that if she plays her cards right, Charlie may well invite her to join the family there. What's more . . .' She leaned towards Lizzie. 'They've an apartment in New York. I knew, I just knew, we were right to get in with them. I've always wanted to see the Big Orange —'

'Apple!' James had turned back to face them, his face like thunder.

'Oh. It's you.' Alice regarded him with surprise. 'Sorry, what did you say?'

'I said,' James remarked with false politeness, 'that it's the Big Apple. New York. Not orange.'

'Whatever,' Alice replied shortly. 'And after all I've done for the mast campaign – did you know I'd got eighty people to write letters? *Eighty!* So they do owe me and —'

'The apartment,' James interrupted curtly, 'is not theirs. It belongs to the company that employs Mr Bingley. So I think your holiday plans will be going on hold.'

And with that he turned and walked away.

Lizzie was standing in the doorway of the marquee, working out just why she was so furious that James had seen her mother yet again at her very worst, when Caroline sidled up to her, her boobs practically bursting out of her low-cut neckline.

'God, that band are so mediocre,' she said. 'Last week, we were all up in London at Geneva Carlton-Grey's coming-out ball, and she had Sky High Groupies as well as i.c.y.'

Lizzie knew she was meant to be impressed so she deliberately said nothing.

'Thank God Emily didn't invite that awful George this evening,' Caroline went on, eyeing Lizzie closely. 'Shows she has some sense – I'd heard a rumour that she was going to ask him because you are keen on him. But of course, I can't believe that even you —'

'Who told you that?'

'So you don't deny it? Well, let me tell you something. That guy is seriously bad news. If you knew how he'd treated James – well, you'd never give him a second look.'

'So, what did he do exactly?'

'Oh, I don't know all the details – it happened when I was away at school and James isn't one to talk about things that upset him.'

'I bet he's not.'

'But one thing I do know: George is not the kind of person you want to hang out with. He can't be trusted – James told me that.'

'And I'm supposed to trust his word? I don't think so.'

'Suit yourself.' Caroline shrugged, her eyes narrowing. 'But if you want to be friends with us, you'll keep well away from George. Your choice.'

'I have never heard such an arrogant, pompous . . .' Lizzie began, but Caroline had already drifted away towards the chocolate fountain.

For the next ten minutes Lizzie stomped round the grounds, tossing her mobile phone from one hand to the other and wondering whether this would be a good time to text George. After all, it would surely be OK to show concern for his friend and to ask if he was all right. She had just begun keying in the first few words when she spotted Jane sitting on a seat by the ornamental pond. On her own.

'Hey, where's Charlie?' she asked.

Jane smiled. 'He and James have gone to check on the results of the cricket,' she replied. 'What is it with guys and sport?'

She got up and let out a sigh.

'What's up? You and Charlie haven't had a row, have you?'

Jane shook her head emphatically. 'No, it's nothing like that – Charlie's going away on Monday,' she blurted out. 'To Italy.'

'I know, Emily said,' Lizzie nodded. 'I don't suppose he's asked you to go along too?'

'That's the whole point,' Jane said. 'Between you and me, I thought he might, I really did. He hinted at it when we were at the races and he sent me a text the following day, checking that I didn't have any plans for the next couple of weeks.' She paused. 'But then – well, I haven't seen him all week, and this evening . . .'

'What?'

'He's been quite distant – not nasty, or anything – he'd never be like that, but not as full on as usual. I think I must have done something to upset him.'

'Jane, why do you always assume it's your fault?' Lizzie demanded. 'Have you asked him outright?'

'I asked if he was looking forward to going away,' she said. 'He just said it couldn't have come at a better time.'

'Oh, Janey. I'm sure he meant that what with his dad being ill . . .'

'Yes, that's probably it,' Jane said. 'Mr Bingley's out of hospital now and he'll be with them. I'm sure that's what Charlie meant.'

Lizzie wished she sounded a little more convinced.

Charlie didn't say goodbye to Jane. The Bingleys left the party well before the end and Jane, assuming there had been a problem, had immediately sent texts to Caroline and Charlie asking what was wrong.

On Monday, she got a text back.

Landed at Pisa. Hot and sunny. Back late September. Caroline.

And that was all.

'He'll ring tomorrow,' Lizzie assured her sister. 'Probably waiting to be on his own so he can chat.'

'Probably no signal at the villa,' she said three days later, as she caught Jane staring disconsolately at her mobile. 'Have you checked your emails?'

'Maybe he didn't take a laptop,' she suggested at the end of the first week.

'Maybe,' Jane said, 'he just doesn't like me as much as I thought he did.'

'Well, if that's the case, he's a fool,' Lizzie retorted.

'Treating you like that.'

'Be fair, Lizzie,' Jane said. 'He hasn't done anything wrong. I'm the one who misread the signals. Let's just forget all about it, OK?'

'You know something?' Lizzie remarked. 'The more I see of guys, the less I understand what they're for. Strikes me we can get on very well without them.'

PART TWO

CHAPTER 11

'You must allow me to tell you how fervently I admire and love you.'
(Jane Austen, *Pride and Prejudice*)

LIZZIE PEERED OUT OF THE WINDOW AS THE AIRCRAFT banked and began its descent into Rodez airport. Now that the moment of truth had arrived, she felt nervous. What if she didn't fit in at the Lefevre Centre? What if the other student on placement was a far better musician than she was? What if her mother was right and all her ideas about the future were just pipe dreams?

In an attempt to ignore the turbulence as the plane hit a layer of rain clouds, she cast her mind back to the day her A-level results arrived. A for French, A for German, A for music, B for Spanish. The only one that really mattered to her was music. But while she had been over the moon to have achieved her goal, she knew that the real challenge was about to begin.

'What do you mean, you're not going to university?' Her father had been sufficiently astonished to drop his new score of *Love and Other Demons*. 'With results like that, of course you are. Any university worth its salt will snap you up . . .'

'She's premenstrual,' her mother had assured him, mouthing the words. 'She'll see sense tomorrow. It's all planned. Of course, she's going to uni.'

'Mum, stop it. It's not like I'm going to be a dropout.'

'Well, of course, that Vanessa Mae's done very well, and if you were to play at the Albert Hall, and maybe make a CD or two that hit the top ten . . .'

'For heaven's sake, Mum! I'm going to try for the Guildhall School of Music and —'

'Now wait right there!' her father had said. 'Darling, I know you sing beautifully, and we're very proud of you, and you've had huge fun with the wind band as well . . . but it's a cut-throat world, the music industry, and only a handful make it to the top and whatever your mum may think —'

'Dad, will you listen?' Lizzie had burst out. 'I don't want to be a professional singer. I want to get the degree so I can go on and do a Masters in Music Therapy and then work with brain-damaged children or —'

'Lizzie!' her mother cried. 'There's no money in that sort of career and —'

'Why does it all come down to money?' Lizzie shouted. 'I don't care about the money!'

'That's all very easy for you to say now that we've got plenty of it,' her mother retaliated. 'You weren't brought up the way I was – hand to mouth, not being able to go anywhere, do anything.'

Of course, that had made Lizzie feel terrible. She knew that her grandmother had struggled to raise her mum and aunt on her own, and understood that being hard-up was the one thing Mrs Bennet would never want to experience again. But she stood firm. She knew that she might never make it, but she also knew that if she didn't give it her very best shot, she would never be able to live with herself.

In the end, her parents had agreed not to discuss the matter again until Lizzie returned from France. She was sure they were hoping that a few weeks working at the LeFevre Centre would make her see things differently.

'They might be right,' Jane had ventured to suggest the day before, as she was packing to go back to university. 'I mean – won't it be awfully depressing, seeing all those kids with autism and learning disabilities and stuff?'

To be honest, Lizzie wasn't sure how it would be. She just knew that when she sang, even the worst day got better; and that even at Meryton Academy, she'd seen some of the most disruptive Year 7s respond to rapping or venting their frustrations on a drum kit. She knew that a child who couldn't or wouldn't speak would suddenly start humming to a tune as they bashed a xylophone and that kids in a coma responded to their favourite chart hit.

'Please remain in your seats with your seat belts fastened until the aircraft has come to a complete halt.'

This is it, thought Lizzie, pulling her mobile from her pocket as the plane's wheels hit the tarmac.

Landed! she texted to Jane. Her fingers hovered over the keys. *Hope you're feeling better*. No, that wouldn't do, because if she was, it would just remind her of Charlie and that would be fatal.

Miss u already – email me every day or else!

She clicked Send and began keying another message.

Hi George! Just landed at Rodez. Miss u . . .

No. This was silly. She had seen George several times after he got back from London, but then he'd gone dashing off to London again and she hadn't seen him for two weeks. He said he was job-hunting, but Emily, who had been to London to visit her grandmother, caught sight of him in the King's Road. With a girl.

She could have just been a friend. Or a relative. Or not.

Hi! Just landed. Tried calling you loads before I left but no reply. Ring me when you get this. Was that too keen?

Oh, what the hell, she thought. I do miss him. And I want to know where he is.

And why he hasn't phoned in ten days.

To: JaneyBen@ntlworld.com
From: LizzieBen@ntlworld.com

Where shall I begin? This place is amazing. A huge country house – the kind you see in costume dramas about Marie Antoinette! The whole of the ground floor is kitted out with music suites and therapy rooms and in the grounds are lots of bungalows for families to stay in while kids are getting therapy.

My room is in the stables (they've been converted!) – and luckily I don't have to share. Only one downer, though; the other girl on placement isn't coming – she's got glandular fever. But I reckon there won't be much time to feel lonely or homesick; I've been given my schedule and it's pretty full on. Which is just as well – at least I'll be able to tell Drew that I'm too busy to meet up if he tries to get in touch!

She glanced at the map pinned to her bedroom wall. The LeFevre Centre was a couple of kilometres from Figeac, and the hotel were Drew was working was just nine kilometres away. Rather too close for comfort.

How's uni? Is it good being back in London? Bet you don't miss working at the café!! Have you . . .

At that point, Lizzie paused, her fingers hovering over the keys of her laptop. Should she ask whether Jane had heard from Charlie or would that just reawaken old wounds? The Bingleys had been in Italy throughout August and most of September, but Lizzie guessed they must be home now – after all, Charlie would be in London starting work at his uncle's estate management firm, and Caroline was due to start at some upmarket college in Kensington. Then again, if she asked the question and Jane hadn't seen Charlie . . .

She deleted the last two words and sent the message. If Jane had any news, Lizzie knew she would be the first to hear it.

To: LizzieBen@ntlworld.com
From: JaneyBen@ntlworld.com

Hi! So glad you're settling in – how's the work? I really miss you. It's been a horrid week and there's no one I can talk to about it except you. My friends here have never met Charlie and – well, sorry in advance if this email is full of moans.

Where shall I start? The Bingleys are back. Vanessa and Edward (Charlie's father) are at Netherfield and she and Mum went with some others to the council meeting about the phone mast.

Big hoo-ha about that – Mum thinks she'll make the newspapers! – but I'll fill you in on it later. Anyway, Vanessa told Mum that because of Mr Bingley's need for rest and recuperation, they've decided to rent out the house for three months to friends from New Zealand and go back to Italy. So Charlie won't be coming at weekends. Not that it matters. I wouldn't be home much anyway. And even if I was, after what happened yesterday, there'd be no point.

I was walking down Gower Street and guess what? I saw Caroline on the other side of the road with a couple of girls. I went over, of course, and honestly, Lizzie, if looks could kill, you'd be flying home to my funeral. She was so miffed to see me – really up herself, and not at all like she was in the summer holidays. (I know that right now you're raising your eyebrows and muttering that you always said she was stuck up, but honestly, she was fine with me.) Anyway, I asked if Charlie was OK and she said he was having a ball – he and James have rented a flat together. (Caroline went to great lengths to tell me it was in one of the best roads in Chelsea!) James is doing his MA and Charlie's out partying every night. With Jenna. James's sister.

She emphasised that bit of the conversation three times. 'Charlie and Jenna, Charlie and Jenna . . .'

And you know what? As I was walking away, I saw James coming out of a shop – Caroline said something to him, he looked my way and just turned his back and they all laughed.

So that's it. Charlie obviously doesn't miss me and he doesn't want me.

Lizzie paused in her reading of the email. It didn't make sense. She'd seen Charlie and Jane together, and she knew beyond a shadow of doubt that Charlie really fancied her, loved her, even. Besides, George had told her that Jenna was a stuck-up, manipulative, dangerous girl and she knew that Charlie wouldn't be attracted to someone like that.

She sighed, and continued reading.

Everyone else is fine. Meredith's column in the paper was a hit – I've sent it as an attachment to this. And guess what? Lydia's been invited to go to Cornwall for half term! Apparently Mrs Forster's new man has a huge holiday home near Newquay – he's hoping to turn it into a boutique hotel – and he's told Amber she can take a crowd of mates. Katie's in a real strop because Amber hasn't invited her. Tim, Denny and his new girlfriend (did I tell you Lydia's gone off him?) and George are all swanning off.

Lydia in Newquay with Amber? The mind boggled. And George? Well at least she knew where he was. She'd phone tonight.

George is working at the Leisure Club at the moment while he looks for a permanent job – but I guess you know all that now – he'll have rung you and you'll know more than me!

I wish. Why hasn't he rung?

Last bit of news – Emily is going out to France!! Apparently, Drew's got her a job at the hotel – only waitressing, I think, but since she fluffed her A-levels and doesn't have a clue what to do, she's taking it. She's over the moon about being near you; says she has loads to tell you. And she really seems keen to be with Drew – no accounting for taste! But then again, not being with someone you care about is pretty grim.

Lizzie, I miss Charlie so much. I keep being tempted to text him or send an email, but I mustn't. I'm not going to let this hijack my life. From now on Charlie Bingley is history. I won't mention him again.

And you mustn't either. It's over.

Lol, Jane

Lizzie switched the laptop off and snapped it shut. Grabbing her French horn and a pile of sheet music, she headed down the twisting staircase and across the courtyard to the main building. She wanted to wring Charlie Bingley's neck. How could he dump Jane like that? And for some twit of a kid who dabbled in drugs and probably was simply out for all she could get.

She stopped dead in her tracks. James. This would be his doing. James wanted Charlie to get it together with Jenna, so that he'd forget Jane. It was all becoming crystal clear – James knew that Lizzie had heard all the facts, the whole truth about his foul behaviour, from George. Knew that he'd done the dirty on a supposed friend, someone who had been doing all he could to stop this Jenna from making a total mess of her life. And he probably had the sense to know that Lizzie would have discussed it all with Jane. And if Jane got the chance to tell Charlie about it . . .

James didn't want Jane and Charlie together because he wanted Charlie to fall for Jenna and by falling for Jenna, keep the whole dirty secret quiet. Put his own spin on it, cover up what he'd done.

Because of James Darcy's arrogance and deceitfulness, her sister was going to hell and back.

She couldn't prove it, of course. Which meant that there was absolutely nothing she could do about it.

The next week was so busy that Lizzie had little time to think of anything that might be going on at home. She observed classes, took notes, played the guitar and sang at all the Rhythm and Bounce sessions; she read loads of books on music therapy from the library in the Centre, and joined *Chansons Célèbre*, the local folk group. Luckily, because kids came from all over the world, English was the main language, but Madame LeFevre was thrilled with her fluency in French and often got her to translate local folk songs into English. In her free time, Claudine Picout, one of the younger permanent staff members, took her canoeing on the Célé river and introduced her to truffles and saffron in a bistro in Marcilhac. By the following Sunday, Lizzie had fallen in love with Figeac-Cajarc and decided that only one thing would make it totally perfect. George.

One evening, she received a lengthy email from Drew, informing her that not only was Katrina De Burgh at the hotel for the next couple of weeks to oversee the first influx of guests, but that she was singing his praises to anyone who would listen, and that because of his influence, Emily (actually he referred to her as 'the gorgeous Emily', which Lizzie felt was poetic licence taken a step too far) had been given a job as a waitress.

A day after this email, as she was struggling to transpose a French folk song into a key that would be suitable for her voice, her mobile rang.

George! she thought instinctively. But it wasn't George, it was Emily.

'I'm here and it's great,' she babbled. 'And I so want us to meet up – I've heaps to tell you. How do I get to you? Or can you come here?'

'I don't know,' Lizzie said. 'I have Tuesdays off, but I haven't a clue about buses or anything and it's too far to cycle. I'll sort something and ring you back.'

As it happened, it was all sorted for her. Madeleine LeFevre, the director, called Lizzie into her office the following morning, told her how pleased she was with her progress and assured her that she would write a glowing reference to go with Lizzie's application to the Guildhall School of Music.

And then she mentioned the dinner.

'It is to raise funds for the Centre,' she informed Lizzie in her impeccable English. 'It will be held at the *Château de la Belle Rose*, a new hotel – once the home of a very dear friend of mine.'

'The *Château de la Belle Rose*?' Lizzie repeated. 'The one at Balaguier?'

'You know it?'

'I have friends who are working there,' she replied. 'In fact, I wanted to go and see them, but I haven't a clue how to get there.'

'*Merveilleux!*' Madeleine cried (she always reverted to French when excited). '*Alors, cet après-midi nous irons . . .* This afternoon we will go together. I have arrangements to make and you can visit with your friends.' She beamed at Lizzie. 'And you will then prepare the entertainment for the *soirée*,' she declared. 'It will be for you the good experience, no?'

'The children will be allowed to play music?' Lizzie gasped, thinking what an amazing step forward that would be. 'Lucien could show off on the drums – he'd love that, and maybe Jules . . .'

'Not *les enfants, ma petite* – I'm afraid the guests would not be up for that. No – you!' Madeline laughed. 'You will sing to the guests. You will be the cabaret.'

'I can't do that,' Lizzie gasped.

'You can, *ma chère*, and you will. Your voice is beautiful.'

'But . . .'

'But nothing,' she replied. 'I have decided.'

'Oh, wow!'

Lizzie stared out of the window in amazement as Madame LeFevre drove slowly up the driveway towards the hotel. The building stood on a hill overlooking manicured gardens and a large shimmering lake. In the late afternoon sun, the stone walls glowed like toasted caramel, and the slate tiles on the turrets glistened from the recent shower of rain. To one side of the driveway, workmen were putting the finishing touches on the new nine-hole golf course and, beyond a fringe of walnut trees, Lizzie could see two tennis courts and the half-finished roof of a large gazebo.

'I remember when this was a family home,' Madeleine sighed, spinning the wheel and bringing the car to a halt outside the front entrance. 'Jamie and Johnnie used to jump out of the trees and frighten the visitors – *sacré bleu*! The times they have almost given me the heart attack!'

She switched off the ignition, opened the door and beckoned to Lizzie to follow her.

'I will be tied up for a couple of hours, so find your friends and – ah! The dear boys. They are here!'

She ran up the steps, arms opened wide to embrace the two guys standing at the open doorway.

Lizzie froze on the spot. Beaming with delight at Madeleine was a tall ginger-haired guy she didn't recognise. And a dark-haired one she knew only too well.

James Darcy.

Like a film going backwards at fast speed in her head, it all clicked into place.

Auntie Kay's in France . . .

James is in a sulk – he should be in France at the family chateau . . .

At that moment, James looked up and caught her eye. It gave Lizzie a certain frisson of pleasure to see just how wrong-footed he was by what was clearly her totally unexpected appearance.

The ginger-haired guy introduced himself as Johnnie Fitzwilliam, a cousin of James who, as a junior partner in a firm of architects, was involved in the renovation of the chateau. 'I've heard heaps about you.'

'Really?' Lizzie frowned, following them into the hotel foyer.

'Oh yes, James was talking about you only yesterday.'

'In which case you'll probably have heard all of my faults and shortcomings – James doesn't like me.' Lizzie laughed, noting with amusement that James had stopped dead in his tracks and was eyeing Johnnie with obvious irritation.

Johnnie grinned. 'Right now, I don't reckon he likes anyone very much,' he replied, dropping his voice as James turned to speak to Madeleine. 'He hates the chateau being turned into a hotel – which I guess is understandable. It's kind of the last link with his mother – it was her parents' home, originally, you know.'

'I didn't know that,' Lizzie murmured.

'And Auntie Kay made sure it was bequeathed to her – horrid arguments after her death about that. Still, all water under the bridge now.'

He sighed. 'James loathes change of any sort, you know – hates the new golf course, thinks Auntie Kay is out for money, money and more money . . .'

Before he could say any more, a side door opened and a tall, elegantly dressed woman in a gold and brown silk kaftan and matching turban crossed the hallway and kissed Madeleine on both cheeks.

'Madeleine, so good to see you again!

'And you, Katrina – looking as always wonderful!'

So this was the famous Katrina De Burgh, James's aunt. And Drew's boss.

As if summoned up by the very thought of him, Drew

appeared from the same doorway.

'Drew, good to see you,' Lizzie lied. 'Is Emily —'

'Not now, Lizzie,' he hissed. 'I'm working.'

He sidled up to Katrina.

'Mrs De Burgh – the briefing for the new waiting staff . . .'

'Yes, yes, Andrew, what about it?'

'Well, it's five o'clock and I assumed you'd want to be there and —'

'Andrew, if you are not capable of briefing a handful of staff on how to wait at table, then I'm disappointed in you. You're not here for the good of your health – now get along and deal with them.'

'Of course, Mrs De Burgh, absolutely, Mrs De Burgh . . .'

Avoiding Lizzie's amused but sympathetic glance, he hurried back the way he came.

'That guy is seriously stupid,' James commented. 'Why on earth is he here, Auntie?'

'I owe his stepfather a favour,' Katrina replied. 'And the biggest one I could think of was to remove the boy for a few months. Now, Madeleine, do come along and have an aperitif and we'll discuss this concert.'

'Before we start,' Madeleine said, 'meet my cabaret! Lizzie sings like an angel and she's going to – oh dear, what is the English word? – she will bring the room down?'

'Bring the house down,' laughed Katrina, shaking Lizzie's hand. 'I look forward to it.'

'You should,' James cut in solemnly. 'She does have a beautiful voice. I heard her sing at a church choir festival last month.'

'You were there?' Lizzie gasped.

James smiled. 'I was. You were the only thing that made it worth missing cricket for.'

Before Lizzie could say another word, Katrina butted in. 'Oh, and Johnnie dear, will you just come through and sort out that wretched computer programme for me – I need to show Madeleine the layout for the evening.'

Johnnie grinned. 'It's so easy a five-year-old could do it,' he teased, turning to Lizzie. 'I'll be back in a moment. Don't disappear.'

James turned to Lizzie as Johnnie left. 'It's good to see you, if something of a surprise,' he said. 'I heard you were in France, but I didn't realise you were nearby. Er – um – are your family well?'

'Fine, thanks – who told you I was in France?'

'Er . . .'

'Caroline, I guess,' Lizzie said. 'Jane saw her in London the other day. She told you that, I'm sure.'

'No, why should she?' James replied curtly, turning with visible relief as Johnnie reappeared. 'Johnnie, I'm going to have a swim – are you coming?'

Johnnie shook his head. 'No, I've got to go over to the stable block and check on some work being done there,' he said.

'Ruining another bit of the property, are they?' James sighed. 'Well, I'm going anyway.'

He glanced at Lizzie, took a step towards her and then paused. 'Er – I hope to see you later? At Madeleine's fundraising do, at least?'

'Yeah, right.' Lizzie's mind was racing and she jumped as Johnnie touched her arm.

'Would you like me to show you round a bit on my

way to the stables? Pass the time till Andrew and your friend are finished with their briefing?'

'Great,' she said, aware that James was still staring at her and looking far from comfortable. 'Lead on!'

'This must have been an amazing place to grow up,' Lizzie said, gazing round her at the woods beyond.

'It was,' Johnnie agreed. 'Not that James and I were here all the time, of course. Just in the holidays. He was at school, first in Scotland and then at Heddingfield.'

'Were you there too?'

'Me? Sadly, no – my father didn't approve of co-ed schools – thought I'd be distracted by all those pubescent girls! Of course, it made things worse; I spent all my free time ogling every girl I saw and making disastrous liaisons in the holidays with totally unsuitable types!'

'You sound just like James,' Lizzie said.

'He's not as gullible as me.' Johnnie laughed. 'Not one to hurl himself headlong into a relationship – in fact, the opposite. Very cautious is our James, takes an age to trust anyone. And from what he was telling me on the way back from the airport yesterday, he's just saved his best friend from making a total fool of himself with some girl he hardly knows.'

Lizzie's stomach lurched. This was her chance to uncover the truth. Not that it was rocket science; Jane had said James had seen her, and James had said he hadn't. And she knew who she trusted.

'His best friend?' she asked as casually as she could.

'Mm – Charlie Bingley,' Johnnie said. 'They met at uni – same college.'

'Do you know this Charlie?'

'I've only met him once – seemed a nice guy, actually – and certainly James and he are like this.' He held up two crossed fingers. 'Anyway, this Charlie took up with some girl – really pretty and quite bright, James said, but she was the type who just couldn't be trusted – we've all met them, haven't we? – and the family! You should have heard him mimicking them – raucous sister, you know, a real chav! And the mother – it was a scream.'

'Was it?' Suddenly the sun seemed too bright and the sparkles from the lake felt like needles piercing her eyes and making them water.

'You know what James said? He reckoned they'd won the Lottery —'

'Gosh, is that the time?' Lizzie burst out, determined not to cry in front of him. 'I ought to go and find Emily – I'm sure she must be out of her meeting by now.'

'Probably – look it's been jolly nice meeting you and —'

'Yes, great. Thanks!' Lizzie broke into a run, her heart pounding. How dare he! How dare James say that Jane couldn't be trusted – she was the most trustworthy, caring person in the world. His criticisms of her family were bad enough but at least she could see where a snob like him was coming from – but to slag Jane off! He was without doubt the most vile, hateful, despicable rat she'd ever met.

That settled it, she thought. I am never, ever going to speak to him again. Never, that is, after I've told him precisely what I think of him.

And the sooner the better.

* * *

Lizzie didn't see any more of James that evening. It had taken Emily a full half-hour to calm her down and it was only when Drew appeared with a platter of cheese, grapes and baguettes and a bottle of wine (about which he launched into a detailed description, assuring her that he was becoming *au fait* – he pronounced it 'oi fete' – with the local vintage) that she relaxed and began to enjoy being with her friend.

'He's a bit up himself, I know,' Emily said, after Drew had disappeared to replenish the grapes. 'But you know what? Here I am – in France, with a job and a load of fit guys from the village who come to work here every day. I get loads of free time, Dad's given me enough euros to feed an army and Drew's – well, he really fancies me, makes a fuss of me and at last, I'm like everyone else. I've got a guy.'

'Not everyone has,' Lizzie said. 'Me, for one.'

'Your fault and no one else's,' Emily reminded her. 'Just because the guy doesn't yet exist who would be good enough for you . . . although I really thought James had a thing about you.'

'Emily,' said Lizzie. 'Steer clear of any more wine. It's affecting your brain.'

Two days later Lizzie was in her room reading online, with open-mouthed amazement, the *Meryton Chronicle*'s account of the latest council meeting. One Mrs Alice Bennet had stood up and chastised the council's planning department for its 'shortsighted and arrogant disregard for the health and wellbeing of the county's children'.

Just then there was a knock on the door. Opening it, she was astonished to see James standing there.

'I know I shouldn't be doing this,' he began.

'It's OK, I'm off duty,' Lizzie said, stepping back to let him into the room and gesturing towards the one available chair.

'I didn't mean that,' he said. 'I'm about to do something that I'll probably regret, but I just can't help it.'

He took a deep breath.

'I know it's crazy, but I just can't get you out of my head. Ever since that evening at the Bingleys when you argued like someone possessed, I've tried to forget you. And I can't.

Lizzie was speechless, which didn't matter much as James was in full flood.

'I admit, I don't get it. You're just not the kind of girl I ever imagined I'd think twice about.'

Here clearly words failed him, but only for an instant. Suddenly, he took a step towards her and grabbed her hand.

'I can't help what I feel. There's something about you, Lizzie – you're fiery and infuriating, but when I'm asleep I dream about you, and when I'm awake I spend all my time trying to get you out of my head because I know it can't work. Our backgrounds are so different, your family are, well . . .'

For a moment he closed his eyes and shook his head as if there were no words to describe what he wanted to say.

'But despite all that, I think I'm falling in love with you, so will you go out with me? Just to see what happens, especially here, where your family are miles away and can't wreck things . . .'

'Stop right there!' Lizzie shouted, pulling her hand away. 'I knew you were pompous and self-opinionated, but this – is this your idea of a chat-up line? Telling me my family aren't good enough when your own father was just a headmaster.'

'He was. He also happened to be the son of one of the Queen Mother's equerries. And my mother was the youngest daughter of the Earl of Barroth. So you see, our worlds are poles apart.'

'So let's keep them that way!' Lizzie spat the words out, her fists clenched as she stormed across to the window.

'But I think we should try.'

'Oh, you do, do you? If you think I'd even consider going out with a guy who has done nothing but criticise me and put my family down, you must be mad. It didn't take me long to realise that you think you're the centre of the entire universe. Well, you're not.'

'I never said —'

'OK, so my family have only recently come into money – that's true. My grandmother cleaned houses for other people so that my mum could go to art college. That disgusts you, I guess?' She didn't wait for him to answer. 'My father – who I suppose in your words was way above her in education and social status, God how I hate that kind of talk! – fell in love with her and married her for no other reason than that she made him happier than any other girl he knew.'

She swallowed hard to hold back tears.

'And yes, she can be embarrassing – but you know

what? She's not half as embarrassing as you because she does what she does out of love. Misguided, maybe, but out of love, while you . . . the only person you love is yourself.'

'That isn't true – I've just said, I think I love you. And my friends —'

'Oh, your friends?' Lizzie cut in sarcastically. 'Judging by what I've seen, your friends would do well to steer clear of you. You think I can forget what you did to my sister and to George. Go on, admit it – you turned Charlie against Jane, didn't you?'

'Well, obviously I did – any good friend would because —'

'*Obviously?* Obviously, because we're new money, as you call it? Obviously, because my parents don't have titles or high flying careers?'

James opened his mouth to reply, but no way was Lizzie going to stop now.

'And another thing – I don't go out with cheats and liars.'

'I beg your pardon!'

'Oh, don't come the innocent with me! I know what you did to George Wickham.'

'Oh, it's all about George, is it?' James flushed scarlet. 'I could see you were taken in by that two-faced oily slimeball. That was another thing that made me think twice about going out with you – I mean, a girl stupid enough to fall for George's lies . . .'

'*Lies?* Are you trying to deny that you got him expelled?'

'He managed that for himself by his devious,

manipulative – oh, what's the point of talking to you? You've clearly made up your mind about me.'

He turned and stared at her long and hard.

'You know something? I'm the kind of guy who says it like it is. I hate pretending and for some stupid reason, I thought you might be the same. I thought that if I admitted to all my doubts, it would be like us starting from a level playing field.'

'Oh, we couldn't possibly do that, James – after all your playing field is a public school one, and mine —'

'Forget it!' As James wheeled round and headed for the door, Lizzie wanted to punch herself in the nose for sinking into such petty backchat.

'We had better pretend this last half-hour never happened,' he said. 'I'm sorry I bothered you.'

And before she could think of a parting shot, he was gone, slamming the door behind him.

Leaving her feeling strangely dissatisfied with the whole encounter.

And even more dissatisfied with her own part in it.

CHAPTER 12

'There are few people whom I really love and still fewer of whom I think well.'
(Jane Austen, *Pride and Prejudice*)

To: JaneyBen@ntlworld.com
From: LizzieBen@ntlworld.com

Thanks for your email and sorry I didn't get back to you yesterday. I had the worst . . .

Lizzie paused and then pressed the Delete button. She couldn't tell Jane everything that had happened the day before; her sister would see through anything other than the complete truth and the complete truth would hurt her like hell. Maybe she'd just stick to telling her about the upcoming charity dinner and the news that . . .

New mail! Her laptop pinged and flashed the message. It was from James. How on earth had he got her email address?

To: LizzieBen@ntlworld.com
From JFDarcy@tiscali.net

Dear Lizzie,
Before you delete this in a fit of temper, please read what I have to say. I won't mention us – not that there is an 'us'. But considering all the accusations you hurled at me yesterday, I think you should at least hear my side of the story.

George's father and mine were really good friends . . .

Yeah, yeah, thought Lizzie, as she scrolled down through the message.

. . . in the school holidays when we went to our house in Braemar he and George came too to help Pa restore the garden . . . played together . . . my father supported him through school . . . and he was my closest friend which was why at first I tried to cover up what he was really like.

Lizzie leaned closer to the screen and began reading more carefully.

He used to bunk off school in the evenings and go downtown where he'd meet up with his old friends from the comprehensive. They were a pretty rough lot . . .

Here we go, thought Lizzie. State school equals yobs in his eyes.

. . . but I told myself that it was just that he missed them (a

lot of the guys at Heddingfield looked down on him and shut him out, if I'm honest) and so I never said anything, even covered for him from time to time. Then one summer, things got really bad. His grades had been dropping, and my father was really worried; Pa had paid for George out of his own money (but of course, being the kind of guy he was, he'd told George it was a full scholarship) – he was so sure he'd be a real high flyer. I tried to talk to George, find out what was going on, tell him how disappointed Pa would be if he blew his chances.

Lizzie paused, irritated to be interrupted as her mobile shrilled.

'Hi, Lizzie, guess what?' It was Emily. 'Guess what?'

'Go on.' Lizzie's eyes were still on the email in front of her.

'I've been made permanent – you know, on the staff,' she enthused. 'Which means I get to stay as long as I like.'

'By which you mean, as long as Drew's here,' teased Lizzie. 'That's great.'

'Yes, but that's only the half of it,' Emily went on. 'Drew says that when he goes back to the States, I can go with him for a holiday, meet his mum and stepdad – do you think that means that – well, you know . . .'

'I think it means that whatever happens, you'll get a great holiday and I'm really pleased for you. Look, I've got to go,' she lied. 'I'm needed downstairs.'

'OK, catch you on Saturday at the charity do-dah. And Lizzie?'

'Mmm?'

'I know you think I'm silly, but I'm really, really happy. See ya!'

Lizzie shook her head in disbelief. How could Emily really settle for a guy like Drew? He was a loser, up himself and totally boring – even Em admitted that. So what was the point? Could her self-esteem really be that low that she'd settle for the first guy to take an interest in her?

She turned back to the screen on her laptop. One phrase leaped out at her.

And then I caught him in the cricket pavilion with my sister.

She brushed her hair out of her eyes and peered more closely.

It was a few days after my father had suffered his first heart attack, so you can imagine the state I was in. I went to the pavilion because I thought it would be empty and I could get myself together before telling Jenna just how ill Pa really was. She was there with George. Suffice to say they weren't discussing the weather. He had his arms round her and . . .

Lizzie swallowed hard. Still, she thought, that was ages ago, and she'd done the same herself with Toby when they were at school. And George had said that he was comforting Jenna because she was upset. What was the problem?

And they weren't just snogging. She had her top off and he was . . . anyway, I was stupid enough to cover that up too.

He said Jenna had been upset about Pa being in the hospital and he was hugging her in a brotherly manner. I knew, Lizzie, deep down, I knew he was lying but I didn't want to believe that Jenna – who was just fourteen at the time – would – well, you know.

Lizzie suddenly felt a surge of – of what? Compassion? Sympathy? James couldn't even express himself fully in an email. What made him so uptight? What had happened to him?

What a blind bloody fool I was! George told me there was nothing going on and I wanted to believe him. Jenna was acting really manic – crying one minute, laughing the next, telling me that I was middle-aged before my time . . . the signs were all there. And I ignored them. Because I didn't want to believe what any other sane person would have known from the start. And then five months later, Pa died. His last words to me were 'Look after your little sister.' I couldn't even get that right, could I?

My father left a large sum of money to George – enough to cover the rest of his education at Heddingfield and three years at uni. You know what he wrote in his will? Well, of course you don't, but I'll tell you. The words are imprinted in my mind for ever. He said, 'I bequeath to George Edward Wickham the sum of thirty thousand pounds, such monies to be used solely for the completion of his education and for his university career. I appoint my son James Fitzwilliam Darcy and my nephew John Edward Fitzwilliam to be trustees together with . . .' and then it was the family solicitor and the school chaplain.

Lizzie was puzzled. If James had actually got George expelled, not only had he done the dirty on a so-called friend, but he'd defied his father's last wish.

I can guess what you're thinking, but please, just finish reading this. God, this is hard. OK. It was a couple of days after Pa's funeral (that was held in the school chapel and I wish it hadn't been because after that, every time I went there . . .). Anyway, we were back at the house we lived in during term time, in the school grounds – Johnnie and Auntie Kay were both there helping out – Johnnie helping, Auntie bossing. Jenna was in a dreadful state, not eating, having nightmares, not even answering texts from her friends. One evening, she said she needed to go and walk her dog. We were pleased – she'd even neglected Spike since Pa's death. We thought she just wanted time on her own out of doors.

Time with him – George – more like.

Lizzie, I won't tell you the state I found her in. Not because I'm sparing your feelings, but because I can't. I can't go there again. You heard Jenna singing on that CD. That is the sound I have to hang on to. When she sings I can believe she's getting over everything that happened. See, that was the night I discovered that George Wickham, the guy you think I've treated so badly – that was the night I discovered he'd been supplying my sister with drugs. How come I found out then? She had a convulsion, was rushed to hospital and nearly died.

Lizzie felt as though everything around her had shifted into freeze-frame. This couldn't be true. George was so laid-back, so confident, so – convincing. She remembered Charlie saying how good it was of James to go to the hospital with Jane, considering how much he hated them; now she understood why.

Again, I can guess what you're thinking – and you're right. George doesn't come across like a drug dealer, does he? A lot of them don't – that stereotype on TV, the unshaven, shifty-eyed idiot in an unlit bar is just that – a stereotype. George's kind are even more dangerous. From what I could gather, he never did drugs himself – alcohol's more his drug of choice. No, that's not true – he snorted a line of coke from time to time, and God knows, that was insanity, but mainly he just supplied others. One of his mates from his old school got him into it . . .

Which is why you have such a downer on state schools, I guess, thought Lizzie, wondering why she had tears in her eyes. You idiot – why didn't you tell me all this instead of acting like some eighteenth-century prig?

He was in it for the money. It happens, I'm told. I wish to God I'd known in time.

So I hope that you will now see that I'm not quite the rank guy you thought I was and that George, despite his amazing ability to convince people otherwise, is out for only one thing. Himself.

Now maybe you can imagine just what it did to me to watch you flirting with him.

Oh, and about your sister. Did you really think that, after I had not only heard her calling out the name of another guy at the hospital and saying she loved him (something that at first I put down to painkillers and a knock on the head) but then, to cap it all, saw her snogging a guy (presumably the same one, although who can tell?) at the races – that I wouldn't warn Charlie he was being two-timed and set up to look a total fool? Charlie's the kind of guy who never thinks ill of anyone and he's been badly hurt twice before by girls who are just out for a good time with a chap who's too generous for his own good. And if it's up to me, it won't ever happen again. So you can tell your sister – she made her bed. Now it's time to lie in it.

James

Lizzie sat motionless for some time, just staring into space. For the moment, George and his lies – if lies they were and deep down she knew they were – faded into the background and all she could see in her mind's eye was Jane in the hospital, and then Simon – the kiss, the slap. Only James quite clearly hadn't hung around to see Jane give Simon what for – he'd only seen the kiss and formed his own conclusions. Could she blame him – really? It must have looked . . .

Her thoughts chased themselves round and round in her head until she wanted to scream.

'What an idiot I've been!' she said out loud to her reflection in the mirror. 'I should have realised – George was just setting me up, trying to make me believe untruths.'

She thought back to the day at the races. What guy would, under normal circumstances, spill his whole life story to a total stranger? Unless he'd wanted to get in quickly with his own version of events.

'I wanted to believe George, for one reason and one reason only – because I'd decided James was an up-himself public schoolboy who didn't give a toss for anyone else,' she admonished herself aloud, glaring at her reflection in the mirror. 'Lizzie Bennet, you're as prejudiced as you thought he was. So what are you going to do about this mess?'

Was there anything she could do? There was only one thing for it: she would have to face James and put him straight about Jane. That way, things just might turn out right for her sister.

'What do you mean, he's not here?'

Lizzie, knowing that she and Madeleine would be at the chateau that afternoon making the final preparations for the dinner the following Saturday, had spent all day rehearsing what she was going to say to James. The thought of not getting the chance to offload was more than she could bear.

'He's gone to the airport to meet his sister,' Katrina told her calmly, handing Madeleine a pile of place cards. 'He'll be back this evening. Have you met Jenna?'

'No,' Lizzie replied, 'but I've heard her sing on a CD. She has a beautiful voice.'

'I'm very fond of her,' Katrina nodded. 'Well, I adore them both, to be honest. Even though James is an obstinate, short-sighted boy at times.'

'He is?' she replied, hoping to encourage his aunt to say more.

'I want him to come into the business – De Burgh

Hotels,' she said. 'Well, it's the least I can do – both his parents are dead you know . . .'

Lizzie nodded.

'And there's a ready-made job for him, great prospects, he could increase his shareholding . . . but will he? No. And do you know why?'

Lizzie shook her head.

'Because he wants to do charity work,' his aunt sighed. 'Can you believe that? I mean, as I said to him, "That's very noble, darling, but you could do a bit of that in your spare time." The hotels could sponsor some little fundraising dos like the one tomorrow night . . .'

She sighed again.

'And do you know what he said? He said that was just paying lip service and he wanted to make a career out of helping the disadvantaged.'

'That's . . .' For a moment Lizzie was lost for words. 'That's just incredible.'

Was this the James she knew and hated? Well, not hated – disliked. Well no, she didn't dislike him . . . oh God. She didn't dislike him. She was beginning to like him quite a bit more than she would have thought possible.

'Incredible? You're right, it's incredible. He's such a softie. As a child, you know, he used to clean my car or do jobs for his father and give the money to any lame duck who came along.'

She shook her head and then suddenly brightened. 'Still, maybe now he's met you – I mean, he does seem keen . . .'

Lizzie felt the colour flood her cheeks as she bit her

tongue and resolved to say nothing.

' . . . but then, no one has ever influenced my nephew. Well, not yet, anyway. I don't suppose you think you could manage to make him see sense?'

Text message!

Lizzie scrolled through Lydia's message the following evening.

Arrived in Newquay . . . great place, all the guys here, so cool! I've got a new boyfriend and he's a dream. Going clubbing now. I'll leave you to guess who it is! Lydia.

Lizzie tossed her phone on to her bed and was about to take a shower when a thought hit her like a bullet from a gun.

If Lydia had ditched Denny, and Amber was with Tim, that only left George. Or Ben. It would be Ben. That was OK. Lydia had remarked about his sexy bum often enough and because Ben had flirted with Katie, it was as good as done that Lydia would want to take him off her. That's who it would be.

'Now Lizzie, you mustn't be overwhelmed this evening,' Drew informed her on the afternoon prior to the charity dinner. 'There will be a lot of VIPs from Figeac and Cahors here and the food will be – well, it will be such as you've never tasted before – and of course, wine will flow and if you're singing you mustn't drink because —'

'Drew, I'm going to be fine,' Lizzie assured him, despite the butterflies slowly gathering in the pit of her stomach.

'I have sung at concerts before, you know.'

'Oh yes, but here – in these sort of surroundings . . .'

'Drew, cut it out!' Emily came over and winked at Lizzie. 'Everything is going to be fine, OK?'

'Well, I hope so, because it will reflect on me, you know.'

'Ah,' said Lizzie with a smile, 'but when someone has had as much experience as you have in the hotel industry . . .'

'You're right.' He nodded, beaming at her. 'Absolutely.'

'Emily,' Lizzie sighed as Drew disappeared through the door from the banqueting room to the kitchen, 'you are a saint. Is he like that all the time?'

'Off and on,' she grinned. 'When he gets on my nerves, there's always Jacques or Leon . . .'

'Emily? Are you telling me . . .?'

'I'm not *telling* you anything,' her friend giggled. 'But hey – this is the first time in my entire life I've had guys to choose from. You think I'm not going to make the most of it? Get real!'

'James, I have to speak to you. It's urgent.'

James's eyes lit up as Lizzie touched his arm as the guests for the charity dinner assembled for aperitifs in the newly restored Orangery.

'Lizzie, I wanted to see you too – I'd like you to meet my sister, Jenna.'

Lizzie turned to see a pretty, raven-haired girl with huge dark eyes and skin the colour of buttermilk looking at her anxiously.

'Hi,' she said, her voice barely above a whisper.

'Jenna, it's great to meet you,' Lizzie said. 'I don't

know if James told you, but I heard your CD and I thought it was stunning.'

Jenna beamed. 'Really? I thought he was stringing me along. You really liked it – you're not just saying that because he told you to?'

'I don't say things I don't mean,' Lizzie assured her. 'And certainly not when I'm told to!' Then, as a shadow crossed James's face, she wished she had chosen different words. 'Tell me about it – how did you come to make it?'

'Well,' Jenna said, glancing at James, who gave her an imperceptible nod, 'I was in this unit – I had a kind of breakdown after my father died . . .'

For a moment she paused, biting her lip.

'Anyway, when they found that music was my thing – I play the harp as well – they encouraged me to join this music therapy class and I started writing songs about – well, all the things that had happened.'

'That's such a coincidence,' Lizzie exclaimed. 'I'm here doing just that – it's a music therapy placement.'

'I know, James said,' Jenna replied. 'Go for it – I can't tell you what it did for me. Even though I'm back at school, I still go to the sessions.'

'Could I see some of the stuff you've written?' Lizzie asked. 'I mean, if it's not an intrusion. I run this choir – Voices Raised, it's called – and I was just thinking . . .'

'Could you two possibly pause long enough for me to get a word in?' James asked pleadingly. 'If we don't go into dinner, Auntie Kay will have apoplexy and trust me, that's not a pretty sight!'

'We'll talk later, yes?' Lizzie said to Jenna.

'Sure, that'd be great.'

'And James? I really need to talk to you too.'

'That was wonderful, Lizzie,' James said after the dinner was over and the guests were dispersing. 'You sing like an angel.'

'There's nothing very angelic about me, I'm afraid,' Lizzie said. 'Can we talk?'

'If you want to.' James sounded doubtful.

'I do. You know what you said, in your email – well, I'm sorry. I'm sorry I got it all so wrong. But there's something more important. About Jane.'

She realised her words were tumbling over one another, but the agitation she felt prevented normal coherent speech.

'You saw her with Simon at the races,' she began.

'Too right I did,' James muttered, raising an eyebrow.

'And you saw him kiss her – NOT her kiss him,' she said.

'What's the difference?'

'The difference is that you clearly turned away so fast that you didn't see her slap him round the face and tell him to get lost,' Lizzie said. 'He came on to her, James, not the other way round. They're finished – they were months ago.'

'Oh, so how come in the hospital . . .'

'She'd had a bump on the head,' Lizzie reasoned. 'OK, I admit, back then she probably still had a bit of a thing for Simon. But she soon forgot him when she met Charlie.'

She paused, offering up a prayer that she hadn't said too much.

For a moment, James didn't speak.

'She never telephoned or sent texts to Charlie on holiday,' he murmured.

'That's not her style,' Lizzie said. 'He didn't ring her and don't say he didn't have her number because . . .'

'He didn't. I deleted it from his mobile.'

Lizzie's mouth dropped open. 'You – you did what?'

'Lizzie! Lizzie, come quickly!' Emily, still in her waitress uniform, came dashing up to them waving a telephone handset.

'It's your dad, and it sounds urgent.'

Lizzie's stomach leaped as she seized the phone. 'Dad?' She glanced at her watch. It was half past eleven at night – what could be wrong? 'Dad? What is it? . . . Lydia's done what?'

At his words, all thoughts of James's deception were forgotten.

'Oh, Dad, no. No. Oh my God.'

'Jenna, go and get a glass of water. Lizzie, sit down. What is it? What's happened?'

Lizzie took a deep breath and tried to compose herself.

'It's Lydia. She's disappeared.'

'Disappeared? What do you mean?'

'She went to Newquay with the Forsters,' Lizzie said. 'A whole gang of them were there. We thought Mrs Forster and her man would be there all the time but the day they arrived, they dashed off to the Scilly Isles.'

'And left the kids alone?'

Lizzie nodded miserably.

'You can guess what happened.' She sighed.

'They had a party?'

'Not just a party – a full-blown rave from what the neighbours say. Someone posted it on MySpace and a whole bunch turned up uninvited and the place got trashed.' She swallowed. 'Amber rang her mother and by the time she got back, the place was wrecked and Lydia and George were nowhere to be seen. And Mr Forster's Smart Car was missing.'

'Dear God!' James breathed. 'Have the police been informed?'

'They rang them straightaway, but at that point they didn't realise Lydia and George were missing,' Lizzie said. 'They do now. Dad didn't phone before because he didn't want to worry me. But it'll be on the TV . . .'

'That quickly?'

Lizzie couldn't keep it in any longer. She burst into tears. 'Yes, that quickly. Because they found a stash of drugs at the house and – oh God!'

'What?'

'Amber says that Lydia is besotted with George and had been acting really wild, and for Amber to say that . . . Lydia is such a fool! She'd act first and think later. If at all.'

James reached for her hand, and she didn't snatch it away.

'I've got to go home, James. I need to be there. You probably think I'm overreacting . . .'

'No, I don't. I think you're quite right. Leave it to me – I'll organise a flight and drive you to the airport first thing tomorrow.'

'That's really kind, but you don't have to,' she protested.

'I do,' he stated firmly. 'I blame myself. If I'd told a few more people about what George was really like, this might never have happened. But now it has – well, we have to do everything we can to sort it.'

'There's nothing we can do,' Lizzie said. 'Except wait.'

CHAPTER 13

'You are too sensible a girl to fall in love merely because you have been warned against it.'
(Jane Austen, *Pride and Prejudice*)

'THIS IS THE NEWS FROM *LOOK EAST*. POLICE ARE APPEALING for help in tracing a fifteen-year-old girl from Meryton and the twenty-one-year-old man she is believed to be with. Lydia Bennet disappeared from a friend's holiday home after a gang of youths trashed a party in Newquay . . . .'

Lizzie had only been in the house ten minutes before the television, which Jane said was almost permanently on *BBC News 24*, flashed a picture of Lydia on to the screen.

' . . . George Wickham is tall with dark hair . . .'

Mr Bennet zapped the remote control and turned to face Lizzie. His face was grey with worry as he paced up and down the room.

'It's been three days now,' he said, his voice flat and expressionless. 'I thought when they found the car yesterday that maybe she'd be nearby. If anything's happened to her . . .'

'The car was OK, there hadn't been an accident,' Lizzie assured him, trying to be positive. 'Jane said that the police guessed it had been dumped when it ran out of petrol.'

'Yes, but I haven't told you the worst bit,' he said. 'Yesterday a text came through. Look.'

He shoved his BlackBerry into Lizzie's hand.

I'm OK but want . . .

'From Lydia? It's not her number – must be George's phone?' Lizzie queried.

'The police said it was – they managed to find out where she was when she sent it but . . .'

His voice broke and Lizzie deduced that the police had been too late.

'And why did she stop? What did she want? To come home? To stay away?'

He paced the room while Lizzie struggled to think of something helpful to say to him.

'I've been a useless father,' he blurted out suddenly. 'Anything for a quiet life, that's always been my motto. And now look where it's got us. If I'd refused to let Lydia run wild so much, if I'd stood up to your mother and told her that she was making things worse. . . '

'Don't be so hard on yourself, Dad,' Lizzie pleaded. 'You're a great father – and Lydia's just going through a phase. She'll settle down when —'

'Lizzie?'

Katie appeared in the doorway, her face even paler than usual and her eyes red-rimmed.

'Can I talk to you? Alone?'

Lizzie was about to protest, but a brief nod from her father was enough and she followed her sister out of the room and up the stairs to her bedroom.

The instant the door was closed, Katie burst into tears. 'It's all my fault, it's my fault,' she sobbed. 'I should have said something, but I thought she was just joking and winding me up like she always does . . .'

'Katie, stop. Nothing's your fault. But if you know something – anything – that might help find Lydia, you have to tell us.'

'Dad will kill me for . . .'

'He won't. What is it you know?'

Katie opened her dressing table drawer and shoved a sheet of lurid pink paper into Lizzie's hands. 'It's an email,' Katie said. 'I printed it off and hid it like Lydia said, but . . .'

We're here! And it's your own fault you weren't invited – Amber knew you couldn't keep a secret and it's taken her for ever to persuade her mum and this new bloke to go off for the weekend so we can rave! But the best bit – AND YOU ARE NOT TO TELL ANYONE YET AND IF YOU DO I'LL NEVER, EVER SPEAK TO YOU AGAIN – George and me are an item! No, really – he says I'm sexy beyond my years – imagine that? He says he fancied me the very first time he saw me in the minibus on the way to the races! Bet if Lizzie knew that she'd go ballistic. George wants us to keep it quiet because he's so much older than me and like he says, it's no one else's business anyway. He is so cool, and so adorable.

Anyway, see you in a week's time! Enjoy boring old Longbourn.

Lyddy.

PS Tell anyone and I'll never forgive you.

By the time Lizzie had finished reading the note, Katie was sobbing uncontrollably. 'What if she's dead? What if something terrible's happened to her? If I'd known it was going to turn out like this, I'd never have agreed to . . .'

'To what?'

'She said that I could go to all the parties and stuff with her and she'd find me a guy, as long as I covered up for her whenever she wanted me to. And I've never been like her, popular and getting to do loads of stuff and now I've messed up and . . .'

'Katie, stop. You've done just the right thing. I'm going to take this note to Dad, and . . .'

'Lydia will kill me.'

'Lydia will thank you one day. Trust me.'

'There's a first time for everything,' Katie muttered, a weak smile flickering across her lips.

Lizzie gave her a hug and ran downstairs. As she did, her mobile bleeped.

Text message.

Let it be Lydia, she prayed.

It wasn't Lydia.

Hang in there. It will get sorted. I promise. James.

She stared at the screen, reading and re-reading his words. That he should have texted her from France – that he should even have been thinking of her when all the time she'd thought of him as a pompous unfeeling snob . . .

For some reason that she couldn't quite work out, his message released all her pent-up emotion. She sat on the stairs and wept as if her heart would break.

And the tears weren't all for her sister.

Once she had wiped her eyes and got herself together she went into the kitchen, drawn by the low hum of voices. Her mother was sitting at the breakfast bar, ashen-faced and folding and unfolding a damp handkerchief; Jane, who had rushed back from uni the day Lydia disappeared, was busily making tea and Meredith was systematically sorting rubbish into coloured recycling bins, only her constant sighing indicating her agitated state of mind.

'Where's Dad?' Lizzie knew that the contents of Lydia's note to Katie would cause all sorts of reactions and she wanted her father to be on hand to deal with her mother's inevitable histrionics.

'In his music room,' Lizzie's mother replied, 'though how he can listen to some stupid opera at a time like this . . .'

Lizzie crossed the hall and peered round the door. Her father was sitting, head in hands, by the window.

'Dad, Katie's got a note from Lydia.'

He leaped to his feet, hope etched in every furrow of his face.

'The mail's come? Give it to me.'

'No, not in the post – she left it behind when she went on holiday.'

'She left – so why the hell didn't Katie tell us?'

He snatched the paper from Lizzie's hand.

'She thought it was a wind-up at first,' Lizzie explained. 'And then, when this all happened – well, I guess she was scared that you'd say she should have stopped it happening.'

Mr Bennet shook his head. 'How could she have stopped it? We all know what Lydia's like when she gets the bit between her teeth.'

He scanned the note a couple of times, and then slumped back down into his armchair. 'It doesn't tell us anything we didn't know or guess.' He sighed. 'Oh, Lizzie, you don't think George and she – I mean, she's under-age . . .'

At that moment, the phone rang. Mr Bennet shot to his feet and snatched the handset. 'Yes? You have? Thank God – is she all right? Of course, of course – thank you, Detective Inspector, thank you!' Tears glistened in Mr Bennet's eyes. 'They've found her. She's safe. But very scared. They're bringing her home now.'

He hugged Lizzie and dashed to the door, flinging it open and shouting down the hall. 'Alice, darling, Jane, Katie, Meredith – they've found her. They've got our Lyddy. She's coming home.'

Never before had anyone in the family seen Lydia so subdued, so shaken and so obviously pleased to be home. The police officers who brought her back were surprisingly gentle with her and very non-committal about the circumstances in which they found her. It wasn't until she'd been hugged to death by all her sisters, and Mrs Bennet had taken her upstairs for a bath that they talked more freely.

'So how did you find her?' Jane asked.

'Was she alone?' Lizzie said at the same moment.

'Let's just say that a couple of people with inside information were prepared to be very co-operative,' the senior of the two officers replied. 'I'm afraid confidentiality doesn't allow me to say more than that.'

'But that Wickham – he'll pay for this, won't he?' Mr Bennet asked.

'Oh, he'll be up on several counts,' the female officer assured him. 'Theft, criminal damage – and if we're not very much mistaken, something even more serious.'

Mr Bennet's face blanched.

'Not – I mean, my daughter's under-age and . . .'

'No, sir. We think George Wickham is a drug dealer.'

'Well, I'll tell you one thing,' Meredith burst out. 'Lydia won't have touched those. We've talked about stuff like that – I used her in one of my surveys at school, and she said that whatever crazy thing she did in life, drugs were for losers and she wasn't a fool!'

Lizzie was touched by Meredith's defence of a sister she normally ignored or criticised.

'We've still to talk about that,' the officer interjected. 'She certainly wasn't firing on all cylinders when we found her, but one thing is quite clear – she's very shaken by the whole experience. Be gentle with her.'

He glanced at his watch. 'We must go,' he said. 'You'll be hearing from us when Wickham comes up before the court. Until then, just enjoy having your daughter home.'

He paused, hand on the door knob.

'And Mr Bennet?'

'Yes?'

'It's good to see such a united family. A lot of the

teenagers we see in trouble don't have a place like this to come home to. She'll do fine, just as long as she's got you.'

'Jane, can I come in?'

Lizzie peered round Jane's bedroom door late that evening after Lydia, exhausted and tearful, had gone to bed with Katie ministering to her like an adolescent Florence Nightingale.

'Sure – I'm nowhere near being able to sleep. Isn't it wonderful to have Lydia home? I'm so happy.'

'Well, here's something else to cheer you up,' Lizzie smiled. 'It's about Charlie.'

'Oh. We said we wouldn't talk about him any more.'

'I know,' Lizzie admitted. 'But I've found out why he suddenly switched off from you.'

'What do you mean?'

'James saw you kiss Simon at the races. Sadly he didn't see the slap, he thought you were two-timing Charlie and so he told him you couldn't be trusted.'

'And Charlie believed him?' Jane replied, far more calmly than Lizzie had anticipated. 'In which case, he never really knew me, did he? Come off it, Lizzie, if you were Charlie, wouldn't you have confronted me, asked me to tell my side of things? I can't see you just accepting it and walking away.'

'True,' Lizzie sighed. 'But perhaps . . .'

'Perhaps nothing,' Jane replied. 'Perhaps we had better just drop the subject. This time for good, OK?'

'If that's what you want?'

'It is, Lizzie. It really is.'

* * *

'This is the first time we've been on our own since you got back,' Lizzie remarked to Lydia a couple of days later. Now that the crisis was over, Jane was back at uni, Katie and Meredith were at school and Lydia, due to return the following day, was sitting in the kitchen nervously picking at the sleeve of her sweater.

'I know what you're going to say,' Lydia replied, showing for the first time since her return a flash of her old stroppiness. 'You wanted George and it was me he liked – only he didn't really, he was using me and . . .'

'Lyddy, stop right now,' Lizzie said gently. 'I didn't want George. OK, I admit, I flirted with him a bit, but there was never anything there, not really. You do promise me nothing happened between you, don't you? If it did you can tell me . . .'

'Like that was going to happen,' Lydia snapped. 'I'm not that much of an idiot and besides, George was so out of it that . . .' She stopped in mid-sentence, clearly aware that she had been about to incriminate herself.

'So how did you get into this mess in the first place?' Lizzie asked.

'It all started as a bit of a laugh,' Lydia replied. 'I didn't know George had put anything about the party on MySpace – not that Amber believes me. She says she'll hate me for ever for what happened to that house.'

'She'll come round,' Lizzie said. 'Dad's going to see Mrs Forster tomorrow to explain it all. And hopefully to tell her what a fool she was to go off and leave a houseful of teenagers on their own.'

'She's a bit odd, actually,' Lydia admitted. 'You know,

she acts like she's thirty, tries to talk in street jargon, brags about knowing all the chart hits. Not a bit mum-like, if you know what I mean.'

'I know exactly what you mean.' Lizzie smiled. 'You've never said what happened after you and George left the party.'

'I told Mum,' Lydia replied. 'And the police. I didn't want to tell you or Jane.'

'Why not?'

'You'll hate me, and I don't want you to hate me,' Lydia burst into tears.

'Silly,' Lizzie laughed, giving her a hug. 'First Katie thinks Dad'll hate her, then you think I will. We Bennets don't do hate.'

'You hate James,' Lydia retorted, sniffing and wiping her eyes with the back of her hand. 'When he caught up with us and the police were taking George away he said —'

'James was with the police? When they found you?'

'James was the one that found us, with some other guy who tipped him off,' Lydia replied. 'And James said that you hated him and had every right to, or something bizarre like that.'

'I don't believe . . .'

'Oh my God, Lizzie!' Lydia gasped. 'I shouldn't have said that.'

'Why?'

'James made me promise – he made the police promise too. He said he didn't want anyone to know he'd been involved.'

'I don't get it,' Lizzie sighed. 'He saves you and then wants it hushed up? What's all that about?'

Lydia chewed her lip. 'OK, I'll tell you. But you have to keep it a secret – James will think I'm even more of a messed-up kid if you let it out.'

'Don't worry about James, just tell me,' Lizzie urged.

'Well, when the riot broke out at the party, George said we had to get out of there as fast as possible. I didn't want to go but then things got really scary – broken bottles and guys throwing chairs and stuff and someone fell in the swimming pool – so I agreed. I thought we were just going to clear off till things died down.'

'And George took the car?'

'The keys were on a hook by the front door,' she said defensively. 'And he said it was just to get us to a safe place.' She hesitated. 'He said I was too precious to him to take any chances . . .' Her voice broke. 'And I was stupid enough to believe him.'

Lizzie took her hand.

'Go on,' she encouraged gently.

'It was really late – about three in the morning, I think – and George said it was best to lie low till the following day, because after all it wasn't us that caused the damage,' Lydia went on. 'And that was true – honestly.'

'OK, just tell it like it was.'

'At first it was fun,' Lydia said. 'Next day, George said that the rest of the week was ours to do what we liked with and why should we go back and face the music for something that wasn't our fault. I know, I know, I should have refused there and then, but I was scared too and I thought we'd lark around for a day or so and then come home.'

She paused, obviously waiting for Lizzie's reaction.

'And then?'

'George left the car in a lay-by and posted a letter to Greg – that's Mrs Forster's boyfriend – to say where it was,' Lydia went on. 'At least that's what he told me. The police say there was no letter. By that evening, I was worried.'

'Why didn't you just phone and come home?'

'My mobile was left at the party, and George said he'd lost his. He kept saying where was my sense of adventure and that kind of thing. And I did really fancy him. I felt kind of wild and grown-up.'

'Lyddy, wild and grown-up don't go together. What happened then?'

'George had this amazing idea – I mean, you have to admit, he's really clever. We caught a train and pitched up at the Laurel Grange Hotel.'

'A hotel? What was clever about that?'

'It's a De Burgh Hotel, silly, one of the chain, and George did this huge thing about being a friend of the nephew of Katrina De Burgh – oh, he burbled on like crazy, it was hysterical, we couldn't stop laughing and . . .'

She caught Lizzie's stern look and stopped.

'It's OK, I'll never do it again,' she muttered. 'That stuff – I mean, you feel great for an hour or so, but then I puked my guts up and felt like I was dying and . . .'

'Lyddy, you didn't take anything?'

'He said it'd be fine and . . . I promise, I've learned my lesson. Drugs suck.'

'And then what? Did you and he . . .?' Lizzie let the words hang in the air.

'He wanted to – I thought I did, but when it came to

it, I chickened out and George – well, he had a lot to drink and kind of crashed.'

'Thank God,' Lizzie breathed. 'You're fifteen – he could have . . .'

'Yeah, I know.'

'And then?'

'Next morning, there I was on TV,' she said, with a slight smile that disappeared when she met Lizzie's gaze. 'We left there pretty damn quick, I can tell you.'

'Without paying?'

'We couldn't risk going to the desk and being seen,' Lydia pointed out. 'I wanted to come home then. I told George I'd had enough. I felt homesick – you know what? It was the weirdest thing, but I missed Katie heaps. I really did.'

'She's your twin, it's not that surprising,' Lizzie remarked, although in truth she was fairly astonished herself. 'Maybe you'll be a bit nicer to her now.'

'I have been a bit of cow, haven't I?' Lydia sighed. 'Not that she didn't deserve it half the time, what with —'

'OK, OK, just carry on. George agreed to bring you home.'

'Yes, he said he would and that was cool, but then . . .' She hesitated.

'What?'

'The police believed me, you have to as well,' Lydia blurted out. 'I went to the loo and I found this packet of white stuff in my clutch bag. It freaked me out. I knew what it must be.'

'And George put it there?'

'I didn't have time to ask, because as soon as I got out

of there, he got this phone call.'

'On the mobile he had supposedly lost?' Lizzie snapped.

'He lied,' Lydia admitted. 'And that's what really freaked me. I began to wonder just why he'd do that.'

She picked at a hangnail and eyed Lizzie doubtfully.

'Anyway, that phone call – I know now that it was a set-up. James had organised it.'

'James?' Lizzie frowned, although her mind was racing ahead and she had a fair idea of what her sister was about to say.

'See, he knew apparently that George had been involved with drugs and stuff before – he didn't say how he knew and I didn't ask. And you mustn't mention that – he was really cagey about it.'

'I won't,' Lizzie said. No need, she knew it all anyway. 'Keep going.' She squeezed her sister's hand encouragingly.

'All I know is that there was this guy – Adam, I think he was called – who owed James a favour and who was also a mate of George's. Adam called George on his mobile, pretended he wanted something.'

'Cocaine?'

Lydia nodded. 'George told him to meet him at this diner place in the town. He told me it would only take ten minutes and then he'd get me a train ticket home. When we turned up, there was James. With the police.'

'Oh, Lyddy!' Lizzie leaned forward and gave her sister a hug. 'Thank God you're safe.'

'I thought I loved him, Lizzie,' Lydia whispered. 'More than Denny, more than any guy before. He made me feel special. And all the time he was selling that foul stuff and . . . why was I such an idiot?'

'It's OK,' Lizzie sighed. 'We all fall for the wrong guy from time to time. And let the right one slip through our fingers.'

'Sorry, what was that last bit? What did you say?'

'Nothing,' Lizzie replied. 'Nothing important.'

For the next two days, Lizzie tried to phone James. When she couldn't get through – his phone appeared to be permanently switched off – she sent a text. He didn't reply.

She had just put the phone down after her tenth attempt, when it rang again almost immediately.

'Lizzie, Lizzie, you won't believe it! Oh my God, it's like a dream come true. Charlie and me – we're back together.'

'Jane, that's wonderful!' Lizzie cried. 'What happened?'

'He rang me and said he had to see me urgently,' Jane gabbled, raising her voice against the babble in the Student Union bar. 'And he told me everything. He knows he was silly to listen to James and he said that all through the holiday in Italy, he couldn't get me out of his head.'

'So how come he never called you?'

'I asked him that,' Jane replied hastily. 'He said that after James had convinced him there was someone else on the scene, he decided to back off.'

'Wow . . .'

'But then, he found he was missing me so much that he made up his mind to do everything he could to get me back!'

'It's wonderful,' Lizzie enthused. 'I'm so happy for you.'

'I really am in love this time,' Jane sighed happily. 'I realise now that what I thought I felt for Simon was just nothing compared with this. And guess what? Charlie's coming back to Longbourn next weekend because the people renting their house have to go home unexpectedly and his mum wants him to sort stuff. I'm coming up with him.'

'Brilliant!'

'And so is James.'

'James?' Lizzie squeaked, her heart suddenly racing.

'Uh-huh. He insisted. Said he had something very important to attend to.'

'I wonder what that could be.'

'Whatever,' laughed Jane. 'I suggest you organise a hairdresser, new lippy and a spending spree by Friday evening.'

'But . . . I'm due to go back to France on Thursday,' Lizzie explained. 'I won't be here.'

'Lizzie, you have to be there. What's a day or two one way or another? This could be very important. Got to go, Charlie's here. Bye!'

CHAPTER 14

'He expressed himself . . . as warmly as a man violently in love can be supposed to do.'
(Jane Austen, *Pride and Prejudice*)

LIZZIE HATED TELLING LIES, BUT THERE WERE TIMES WHEN bending the truth just a little was too tempting to avoid. She phoned Madeleine LeFevre and explained that she couldn't get a flight on Thursday, and wondered if since her sister needed time with the family, she could stay till Monday morning, and return then. Madeleine was effusive in her concern for both Lizzie and Lydia and suggested she took a whole week before heading back to the Centre.

Lizzie hung up feeling extremely happy. The call that came through five minutes later, however, put paid to that feeling pretty promptly.

'Lizzie, it's Katrina De Burgh here. Now will you tell me just what is going on between you and my nephew?'

'I'm sorry?'

'Sorry? I should think you are – I really don't understand it. One minute, James is promising to spend Jenna's half-term week here with me; the next, he's disappearing off to England and Jenna tells me his last words before leaving were "I have to see poor Lizzie through this mess".'

Lizzie opened her mouth, but it seemed that the power of speech had left her.

'Jenna told me that one of your sisters was in trouble with the police. Well, of course, I thought she'd got it wrong, she has a vivid imagination, that girl, sweetheart though she is, but then – well, I can hardly speak of it.'

'Speak of what, Mrs De Burgh?'

'I hear from the manager at De Burgh Laurel Grove that the police had been there, making enquiries. Someone saw a girl who turned out to be your sister with a young man and . . .'

There was a long silence. Lizzie's heart was thumping too hard for her to bother to say a word.

' . . . and after they had left, without paying, I may add, the police found drugs in the bedroom. The local paper got hold of the story, and the next thing I know is that it's all over the tabloids.'

Lizzie swallowed hard, thankful that her parents only took the *Daily Telegraph*, but well aware that there were plenty of people who would relish alerting them to every last paragraph in the gutter press.

'This is a disaster for De Burgh Hotels,' Katrina went on. 'We have a reputation and of course, even in France it's public knowledge – it's been mentioned on *News Twenty-four* that our hotel was involved. Our slogan is —'

'Mrs De Burgh, I don't actually care what your slogan is,' Lizzie interrupted, feeling the heat surge to her cheeks as she tried to keep her voice level. 'Not once in this conversation have you asked whether my sister is OK, whether George Wickham harmed her, how she is feeling. Nothing. All you have done is worry about your reputation.'

'Yes, but you have to understand . . .'

'Oh, I understand. I understand that your business is your life.'

'That's right, dear,' Katrina said, clearly trying to retrieve her position. 'And because of that . . .'

'And because of that, I imagine, James doesn't want to be any part of it. Well, I'm with James . . .'

'You mean you and he are an item?'

'No, I don't, not that it is any business of yours. I mean, I agree with his priorities. Helping other people matters more than any high-flown business reputation. And now if you don't mind, Mrs De Burgh, I have to go. I have people to avoid.'

It wasn't until she had hurled the handset halfway across the room that she remembered who she had last heard saying those very words.

'It's me. James.'

For the first time, as she pressed the phone to her ear, Lizzie realised what a sexy voice James had.

'You're not doing anything today, so I wondered – would you spend it with me?'

Lizzie felt a surge of excitement. Not that she was going to let him get away with being so presumptuous.

'How do you know I'm not booked up from morning till night?' she teased.

'Jane assured me you were completely free,' he replied.

'And since she and Charlie are going boating at Barcombe, I thought you and I might go to the seaside.'

'The seaside?'

'Jane said you love the sea.'

'You and Jane have talked a lot,' she laughed. 'And yes, please, I'd love to.'

'Be ready in half an hour,' he ordered, and for once, Lizzie didn't mind being bossed about one little bit.

Throughout the two-hour drive to Norfolk, Lizzie struggled to calm herself. This was ridiculous; the one thing she had never been in her entire life was at a loss for words, and she had always thought small talk was a sign of a narrow life and even narrower mind. Yet here she was commenting on the weather, or a passing road sign, or the music on the in-car stereo. She had to come clean about Lydia's confession, but this wasn't the time. She'd wait till they got there.

'Your aunt said you wanted to do charity work,' she burst out, with a sudden flash of inspiration.

'Really? I thought she was in total denial over the whole thing,' he replied wryly.

'I didn't say she was enthusiastic about it,' Lizzie said laughing. 'But go on, tell me about it.'

'I'm doing International Human Rights Law for one reason and one reason only,' he replied firmly. 'To help in some small way all those people whose rights are ignored simply because they don't possess the words, or the know-how, to fight for themselves.'

'But surely, that's not charity work,' Lizzie reasoned. 'There must be loads of money in that.'

'Get real,' he argued. 'If you were living in a shack in Calcutta, working sixteen hours a day sewing zips on skirts for some toffee-nosed designer in the West, and then someone came and bulldozed your hut because they wanted the land for a call centre, would you know what to do? Or even if you did, would you have the money to pay a lawyer?'

'So, you'd do it all for free?'

'Not exactly,' James admitted. 'Otherwise I'd become a charity case too. No, I want to work for a charity that helps people in those situations and then one day, set up one of my own. I've even got a name for it.'

He blushed and looked at Lizzie out of the corner of his eye.

'Tell me,' she encouraged.

'Law for Life.'

'I think that's the most fantastic thing I've ever heard,' she said. 'I never realised you were like that. I love . . .'

Oh my God, she thought. Oh my God. I nearly said . . .

'I love the idea,' she finished lamely.

As soon as they had parked the car at Holkham beach and were walking along the duckboards through the pine trees to the huge expanse of sand, she stopped and turned to James.

'I can't go on until I've said what's on my mind,' she began. 'I just want to thank you – really thank you – for what you did for Lydia. Coming back from France like that and fixing it so that George got caught out —'

'How did you know about that? I made Lydia promise . . .'

'She didn't mean to let it slip,' Lizzie assured him. 'She was in an awful state – it's been a shock and something of a rapid growing-up for her, you know.'

'And I shouldn't have asked her to keep secrets from her family, I guess,' he said. 'But you know, I didn't do it for her. I did it for you.'

He began walking and she had no choice but to fall in step beside him.

'I know what you said to me when I told you weeks ago that I thought I was falling in love with you, and I know I deserved every syllable,' he said. 'And if you still feel like that about me – well, we'll just call today a one off and . . .'

'Please don't remind me about how awful I was,' Lizzie pleaded. 'I accused you of being up yourself when all the time, I was the one who was jumping to conclusions about you. I'm so sorry – I cringe inside every time I think about what I said.'

'What about the way I behaved to you? God, how could I have been such a total arsehole? All that pent-up anger I had over what George did, and all the worry about Jenna because she was still seeing the psychiatrist guy at that time . . .'

'I wish I'd known, I wish I'd understood,' Lizzie sighed.

'I didn't give you the chance,' James replied. 'All this stupid pride of mine – not letting anyone know that the Darcys weren't one hundred per cent perfect. What's wrong with us all? The Bingleys hiding Geoffrey's breakdown, me keeping quiet about Jenna – Lizzie, I'm so sorry.'

He stopped and took her hand.

'So – what do you think about me now?'

'I think what you did for Lydia was just wonderful and . . .'

He dropped her hand. 'You see? That's why I didn't want you to know I was involved. Now I'll never know whether you're being nice because of that, or because – because . . .'

He faltered. 'Lizzie, is there any possibility you could begin to like me just a little bit? Not for what I did, but for me.'

'Well . . .'

'OK, forget it. I shouldn't have asked.'

'Will you please let me finish? I was going to say that I think there's a pretty good chance I could.'

His face broke into a smile. 'And even more than just like me?'

He cupped her face in his hands. She decided there was no more point in words.

She had never realised that a kiss could last that long.

'Lizzie, are you crazy?' Jane gasped three weeks later, on one of her weekends home from uni. 'I've only just got used to the fact that you're in love with James. And now you spring this on me. Are you sure? Really, really sure?'

Lizzie nodded, her mind darting back to the previous weekend. James had taken her to a concert at Jenna's school to hear his sister play the harp and sing. Afterwards, they'd gone for a long walk and even now, smiling at the bemused look on Jane's face, Lizzie could remember every word of their conversation.

'Did I tell you that Emily phoned from Boston?' Lizzie had asked him. 'She's engaged to Drew. Can you imagine? Not even nineteen and hooked up with a loser like that?'

She had waited for some cutting remark from James, but instead he had taken her hand. 'So – you wouldn't want to spend your time in the company of the same guy, day in, day out?' he had asked, fixing her with his piercing grey eyes.

Suddenly, she had felt as though every fibre of her body had tensed. 'It would depend who the guy was,' she had murmured.

'What if it was me? Don't answer. Listen. I've decided to go to India for a couple of months – it'll help my research for the thesis.'

Lizzie had swallowed hard.

'And I wondered – well, you are on a gap year and I know there won't be any music therapy places, but there are kids out there in some of the sweat shops who go to these schools in the evening and I thought you might like – I mean, on your CV it might look good and . . .'

'It would be wonderful,' Lizzie had breathed. 'But it would cost an arm and a leg and I know Mum's come into money and all that, but what she does for me, she has to do for all the others and . . .'

'You know, I love the way you're all such a . . .' For a moment he had hesitated. 'Such a close family. But it won't cost that much. We can get a cheap flight and stay in . . .'

'I know. De Burgh Hotels?'

'Get real, Lizzie,' he had retorted. 'Am I honestly

likely to swan around in some five-star hotel while the people I'm writing about scratch a living in the slums?'

He had shaken his head vigorously as if to dismiss such a ridiculous suggestion. 'There are hostels, and places you can stay very cheaply. But it'll be really basic, and I guess not your scene and —'

'Hang on, James Fitzwilliam Darcy! Am I hearing you right?' Lizzie had teased. 'If it's good enough for the grandson of – who was it? Some equerry to the Queen? Well, it's good enough for me!'

'You mean . . .?'

'I'd love it,' she had said. 'Yes, please. I'll come. The money from the tuition I've been doing on Saturdays at the music school will help.'

'I never thought you would say yes,' James had gasped. 'I thought . . . well, it doesn't matter. You do know that I love you more than I ever thought it was possible to love anyone, don't you?'

Slowly Lizzie had nodded. 'And I love you too,' she had whispered. 'So much that it hurts.'

'In which case,' James had smiled, 'you must show me everywhere it hurts, and I'll kiss it better.'

'LIZZIE!' Jane's voice burst in on Lizzie's thoughts. 'You're smiling like the cat who got the cream. You really are crazy about this guy, aren't you?'

'Crazy? No, not really. I think I'm more sane than I've ever been.'

CHAPTER 15

'Think only of the past as its remembrance gives you pleasure.'
(Jane Austen, *Pride and Prejudice*)

TWO MONTHS LATER

'JUST THINK, THEY'RE ALL COMING HERE,' LIZZIE'S MOTHER said for the fifth time on Christmas Eve. 'I told you we'd get in with the important people of the village and this – well, it's just the icing on the cake!'

'Mum, it's mulled wine and mince pies for the carol singers,' Lizzie reasoned. 'Not a black-tie ball.'

'You'd think the entire Royal Family were about to put in an appearance,' Lizzie's father muttered, unloading punch bowls from the hire company's boxes and lining them up on the dining-room table. 'Although I doubt there would be as much fuss if they were.'

'But the Bingleys and the Bradbury-Wellses are coming, not to mention that new family at The Grange – and of course, what with my success over the mast . . .'

Lizzie and Jane exchanged amused glances. Once their mother had had a taste of publicity after her vociferous protest at the council planning meeting, there had been no stopping her. When the crane arrived to erect the mast on the church tower, their way was blocked by dozens of parked cars, all of which carried an outsize poster designed by Alice. Radio Meryton had picked up on the blockade, and Alice, in the absence of Vanessa who had been cruising in the Med, had been interviewed on *Drive at Five*. Meredith had written a column entitled *Graduation, not Radiation* about the effects of radiation on the developing brains of the young and the only downside of the whole thing was a headline in the *Meryton Chronicle* which read *Mother of Teenage Runaway in Mast Protest*.

'I'm so excited!' Alice said, folding paper napkins into star shapes. 'Just think, six months ago, we were newcomers and now there's Jane going out – well, practically engaged, really – with a Bingley and —'

'Mum, don't you dare talk like that!' Jane exploded. 'We're not – and even if we were, which we're not —'

'Hang on,' Meredith interrupted, peering at the bottles of red wine stacked on the dresser. 'This wine isn't organic. It'll probably rot your guts.'

'Meredith,' Mr Bennet replied. 'It's Fairtrade, which is what you demanded. It was cheap, which was what I wanted. And it's going to be mulled, which is what your mother decided. Subject closed.'

'And then Lizzie spending New Year in a Scottish castle . . .' Alice continued, as if there had been no break in the conversation at all.

'Mum, it's not a castle,' Lizzie sighed. 'It's just James's grandparents' home.'

'Well, I've seen the photograph and it's got turrets and everything.' Alice sniffed. 'It's almost a castle and anyway —'

She was interrupted by the sound of the front door slamming shut, some high-pitched giggles and the dining-room door bursting open. Lydia and Katie flew in, Lydia sporting huge Santa Claus flashing earrings and a pair of reindeer antlers, and Katie wearing a pixie hat complete with bell and furry boots that played a tinny version of 'We Wish you a Merry Christmas'.

'Hi, Mum, listen, we're off out, OK?'

'You only just got back,' her mother said.

'Yeah, yeah, we came back to tell you we're going out,' Katie said slowly as if speaking to an intellectually challenged five-year-old. 'Ben's taking me skating, and I said Lydia could come along with Rufus. Cool, eh?'

'Rufus?' Lizzie queried, still trying to get used to the new decisive Katie. 'Not that little guy with the sticky-out ears who came round last week.'

'That is, like, so shallow of you,' Lydia sighed. 'He's just so cute and sweet. He's in my class and he only got here from New Zealand last week, and I've taken him under my wing.'

'Good God,' sighed her father. 'Should we inform Immigration?'

'Come on, got to go,' Katie ordered. 'See you at the carols – bye!'

And with that they shot off, giggling all the way down the hall.

'They are,' said Mr Bennet, 'without doubt, two of the stupidest girls in England.'

'Not as stupid as Lizzie,' Mrs Bennet retorted. 'India, indeed. Of all the places a young man with James's money could have taken you . . .'

'Mum!' Lizzie said. 'We've been through all this before. And it has nothing to do with money.'

Alice sighed. 'I know,' she said. 'It's just that – well, I want what's best for you, of course, but . . . well, I love you so much and I'll miss you.'

Lizzie gave her a hug. 'I'll miss you too, Mum,' she replied. 'But just think – no one else in the village has a daughter working on the subcontinent.'

'The subcontinent,' Mrs Bennet mused. 'That *does* sound impressive, doesn't it? Just wait till I tell that Bradbury-Wells woman.'

She glanced round the room, beaming from ear to ear and turned to her husband.

'You know, God has been very good to us, Harry,' she sighed.

'That, my love,' he replied, 'is one of the sanest things you've said in weeks.'